OUTLAW IN THE SKY

By
CHESTER S. GEIER

I0541415

ARMCHAIR FICTION
PO Box 4369, Medford, Oregon 97504

*The original text of this novel was first
published by Ziff-Davis Publishing*

Armchair Edition, Copyright 2014 by Gregory J. Luce
All Rights Reserved

*For more information about Armchair Books and products, visit our
website at…*

www.armchairfiction.com

Or email us at…

armchairfiction@yahoo.com

THE WILD WEST OF THE MARTIAN FRONTIER

The wilds of Mars were open for the taking, and Terrans had come to the red planet in droves, just to have a crack at starting a new life. But those grim pioneer days on Mars formed a lush field for ruthless men, too. And far too often, greed and murder were their accepted methods.

Cory Balleau had come to Mars as a young boy during those pioneer days. Along with his mother and his uncle, they planned to make a fresh start at life in the Martian grasslands. But as the years flew by, he witnessed tragic events that changed his life forever. Before long he was a bitter, troubled young man, greatly skilled with the use of his deadly pyro-gun. His desire to use this weapon nearly drove him to the point of no return; but could the love of a beautiful young woman sway him from the path of revenge and his own eventual self-destruction?

FOR A COMPLETE SECOND NOVEL, TURN TO PAGE 149

CAST OF CHARACTERS

CORY BALLEAU
He had seen much hatred and tragedy on the Martian frontier and just wanted to be left alone. But fate had other ideas.

KAY BATES
It was easy to label her as the spoiled daughter of a rich man, but her inner strength and beauty made her much more than that.

FRANK BATES
He came to Mars with lots of money and dreams of power—a combination that led to the complete transformation of his soul.

MEL DORKEN
A mountain of a man with a beard. He was nothing much more than a skin full of cruelty walking around on two legs.

JOHN BALLEAU
After losing everything in a Terran war, all he wanted to do was come to Mars and start over, which he did—for a while.

NATE GOODROW
As a scout on a half-track train he was a seasoned veteran of the Martian frontier—and a good man to have around.

FRAKE
He was bad to the core. But he did have brains enough to keep one step ahead of any obstacles thrown in his path.

TIP SNEAD
There was a great deal of a snake about this man: the flatness of his face; the coldness of his eyes, and the treachery in his heart.

CHAPTER ONE

THE HALF-TRACK train had spent an entire day crossing the Marsport River, and now that day was over and the train was camped in an area of red grassland on the westward side.

It was a large train and its population ran the gamut from wealth to poverty. There were the great durium-steel atom-powers filled with the fine things treasured by genteel women. There were the smaller gas-durium jobs, battered and dented. In these rode the people whose only possessions of value were their dreams of what lay beyond the swelling Martian hills. There were even the primitive carts drawn by the sloe-eyed Martian *goffs,* and gorged with the pitiful possessions of those who wore tattered clothing but who also had the dreams—and the will to travel a thousand miles over red plains and barren hills to make the dreams in their hearts come true. They had the grimmest faces and the hungriest eyes of all.

There were the unattached gentry—the scouts in the tight purple clothing of their trade, whose eyes were eternally narrowed against the sun and the wind. They were already a part of this new planet. It was an old planet to them and their competence was clearly apparent in every move they made. There were the gamblers, and they were also self-sufficient and competent, but in a different way.

And there were others.

This train was not a train but a moving community. It could take root on any spot at any time and become a town overnight with all the good and evil that goes into the making of a town.

The good women and the bad women—the liquor for men and the milk for children—the people who filled churches and the people who filled the drinking halls—those who dreamed and worked and those who plotted and schemed.

All this was here—even now—in this traveling city, moving out from Marsport to the fertile plains of the planet.

The boy's name was Cory Balleau. He was eleven and he was a part of the rag-tag and the bobtail of the train. The wheezing, gas-driven truck with the broken tread-links belonged to his uncle—John Balleau. The thin-faced woman who rode on the front seat of the truck with the look of fever on her brow was his mother, Faith Balleau.

There was breeding and background in every line of the woman's body. There was the right kind of pride in her bearing, which showed even brighter than the fever that boiled up from the hot *marsplague* eating at her lungs.

And her mark was on the boy; her delicate features were also his—the soft, long lashed eyes—the pure beauty of feature—the face that served as a mirror for the sensitive mind.

The train had come to rest in two sections, each half strung out to form the side of a street. All activity was in the space between. Plastitents sprang up on the red meadow; tents for living—for gambling—for drinking. Atom-charged food cookers were charged and there was sound and color and action and all these things thrilled the boy.

He had been riding all day and there was pent-up energy in his body. He dawdled for a time around the truck.

Then, with a quick look at his bearded, sober uncle, he took three soft steps and was off, flying down the long street, driven by sheer animal exuberance.

Some twenty-five trucks down, the patter of his bare feet lessened and he went slowly past a fine big GM land-cruiser. There was a yellow-haired girl in this truck. He had seen her, fleetingly, on several occasions and once he had spoken to her. But in the train, as in a town, the lines of discrimination had been drawn. There was already cat-town and shantytown and snob-town. Cory Balleau, in his short run had crossed over and was in alien territory. These big double-traction cruisers were as inviolate as mansions on a hill.

The girl was there—leaning out through the window in the back of the truck. The boy dawdled with studied care under the gaze of her bright interested eyes.

The girl said, "Hello. I've seen you."

The boy said, "I've seen you too. My name's Cory Balleau." He drew a design in the dust with his foot.

"Mine's Catherine Bates, but they call me Kay."

There were legs moving in long strides on the other side of the wagon. The legs were clad in boots of fine leather—expensive boots.

The legs came around the rear of the truck and there was a scowl on the face of the man who wore the boots. The man said, "Get on out of here! No chance to steal anything. Get on with you!"

EACH WORD could have been the lash of a whip laid across the boy's back. The liquid eyes widened. He paled and took one faltering step backwards. He stared at the man.

Immediately there was the sound of movement up in the big truck and a woman appeared beside the yellow-haired girl. The woman had plump, cheerful beauty and she was not past her early twenties—about the same age as the man.

The woman said, "Frank! Stop it!" That was all and the man stood with a sullen look, eyeing the boy.

The woman turned to the boy. A gentle smile was there, nestling in the soft curve of her mouth. "Don't be afraid, boy. It's all right."

He stood mute, writhing under this embarrassment. The woman's smile got even softer and she said, "Are you hungry, lad?"

The yellow-haired girl brightened. "Mama—can he have my dessert tonight? Can he?"

Something burst inside Cory Balleau—something wild and agonizing. Tears flooded out and his words were shrill and high. "I'm not hungry, you—you *snobs!* We've got food! We've got more food than anybody! We don't take charity from snobs!"

He whirled away and was gone—blindly down the street. He smashed head-on into something covered with soft purple leather, though hard as steel underneath. But there was scarcely any shock because the steel yielded like a spring, turned on a pivot, and the boy was lifted and swung back on balance and put down again.

A deep voice said, "Easy there, son."

Cory opened his eyes. The face above his was deeply tanned. There were fine lines cobwebbing into the outer corners of the dark eyes.

This fleeting glimpse and the boy was free and again rocketing down the street. When his breathing had become a sobbing battle for air, his gait faltered and he found himself at the far rear of the train.

Here was a magically changed atmosphere—a distinct and different segment of the colorful whole. Rough *cheekawood* counters had already been set up, and the men who crowded around the bottles thereon were of definite mark. The process of the train's stopping was a little like that of water whirling in a pot. As the water slowed, the dregs swiftly and surely settled to the bottom.

The boy looked around, a trifle bewildered. He had never before come this far down the train. But the bewilderment was secondary in his mind. The sting and shame of his encounter with the yellow-haired girl was still paramount. More than anything, he wanted solitude.

He found a certain degree of it beneath the tracks of a supply truck across from one of the crowded liquor counters. Here he stretched full length and pressed his face against the dust and the coarse crimson grass of the prairie.

He wept with an intensity of one who has a pain deep inside—a pain that will not come to the surface but must be burned away, bit by bit, with scalding tears.

It was not the weeping of childhood, but when it was done the sleep that followed was the sleep of the young.

The boy was awakened by a pounding upon the earth. He opened his eyes and—without turning his head—he was looking out at a myriad of legs. The legs were of all shapes and sizes—Martian legs and Terran legs—and were clad in various ways. Before his eyes there were shoes and boots and purple moccasins formed into a hollow circle. But there were no sounds. This seemed strange. His mind questioned the incongruity of so many men crowded into a circle and, at the same time, such a vast silence.

THE SLEEP faded from his eyes and he saw the two men inside the circle—a Terran and a green-skinned Martian. He raised his head.

They bore a similarity, the two men, a great burly Terran with the hair on his face covering everything but cheek-bones and eyes; the cruel-eyed Martian, thewed like a gladiator. Their beards were thick with dirt. Each was in a crouching position; each had his arms bowed outward with hands spread and hooked and waiting like the talons of preying birds. They faced each other and moved in a circle within a circle. They moved cat-like, silent, deadly, and now the boy could see the hatred in their eyes and hear the jerky gusts of their breathing. He sensed the tightness in the air and his mind cringed from it.

The circling ceased, as though by common consent, and the two crashed together and a roar went up from the straining circle. The boy felt the thud of the contact in his own body. He tried to turn his gaze away from the two men, but they were a magnet, holding him.

The two stood locked together, swaying for a long moment, then they broke apart and the fists of the Terran gained an advantage. The fists lashed out like anvils at the end of pistons and there was the soggy sound of flesh being smashed and ground to green pulp against bone. Sticky life-fluid welled over the face of the Martian. He staggered back, shook his head and bellowed like a wounded bull. The Terran dropped back one step and the crouch was gone from his body. He straightened and brought up one leg in a long arcing kick. His boot, with two hundred pounds of force behind it, drove squarely into the other's groin. The Martian doubled over as though ripped in the middle by a battering ram.

His foe leaped forward, locked his fists together and brought them down against the back of the Martian's neck. The effect was that of a sledge hammer arced over in a full swing.

The Martian took the blow and went straight to the ground, landing squarely upon his face. He groveled, and spewed out a green sheen through a nose smashed flat and filled with dirt and flesh.

But it was not over yet. In a frenzy of triumph, the Terran screamed an odd, gargled scream and went into the air. He came down accurately, both boots crashing into the small of the Martian's back.

The Martian's agony squalled out through his lips in a wave of ear tearing sound.

The boy, cowering beneath the truck, was also in agony. Never before had he known anything more violent than a reprimand from his mother. He lay stiff and terrorized staring at the spots of life-fluid that had splashed under the truck and were drying on the back of his hand. He rubbed the palm of his other hand across the spots and they became green streaks on his brown skin.

The boy raised his head as the fallen man bellowed anew. The fallen man stayed prone and rolled across the ground, closer to the wagon. The circle was breaking into savage sound and now the Martian lay on his back not two feet from the boy.

The Terran was still not content. The viciousness within him still demanded more. He crossed the circle and was upon his foe, astride him, with knees on his chest. The boy saw two rigid thumbs poked downward. He saw the look of horror on the Martian's face. He heard the scream and then managed to close his own eyes. But it was too late. The earth pitched and rolled beneath him and he knew they were helping the Martian up and taking him away.

And he knew also, that they were leading a blind man.

He fainted—

THERE WERE arms lifting Cory Balleau and he opened his eyes. There was the face—tanned dark—and the fine cobweb lines, and he could feel the soft purple leather and the steel underneath.

Cradled in two arms, he could look up at the man and hear him say, "Where do you belong, son? Your folks'll be wondering won't they?"

The boy was wondering too, but about something far different. There was a new feeling in his mind and in his body. His mind could not define the difference but it could note the outward signs of change.

Before, he would have smiled at this stranger and said hello and when I get big I'm going to have a shirt like that. But now he lay stiff in the stranger's arms and did not smile. He said, "I'm Cory Balleau. Up at the other end of the train. Put me down."

"My name's Nate Goodrow," the stranger said. He put Cory on his feet. "I'll walk along a piece with you."

"You're a scout," Cory said.

"That's right—one of them. We sort of keep an eye out. I saw you kiting down the trucks and I'm going that way. So when I see you snoozing under that wagon I took notice."

The other Cory Balleau would have been thrilled at walking past the trucks with a scout. They were fabulous creatures from whom one was grateful for a nod or a word.

The other Cory Balleau would have been thrilled.

"Who were those men?" the new Cory asked.

"Oh, you saw that, did you? Thought maybe you'd slept through it. A couple of maintainers." He glanced sharply down at the boy. "Those things—happen," he said.

Cory could see the home truck now. Uncle John had an atom cooker going in front of it and was standing by the cooker looking anxiously up and down the thoroughfare. Then Cory saw Uncle John step back into the shadows and kneel down beside what looked like a deeper shadow.

There was panic in Cory's heart and he was running.

The deeper shadow was a mattress stretched on the meadow ground and Faith Balleau lay on the mattress with John Balleau bending over her, wiping blood from her lips. He looked up…

"Your mother had a hemorrhage—a bad one."

Cory dropped to his knees beside the mattress.

"Mom—Mom!"

Her eyes opened as though by great effort. She smiled and raised a slim white hand and passed it over her son's, tousled curls. "You went away. I was worried."

"I'm sorry, Mom."

John Balleau had moved back and Cory saw that he was talking in low tones to Nate Goodrow, the scout. They talked for some minutes and then Nate Goodrow turned and hurried away. John Balleau came back and knelt by the side of his sister-in-law.

After a while there were footsteps and another man came to the truck. He carried a medical kit and he seemed tired but his voice was not unkind when he said, "You go with your uncle, son. You take a little walk with your uncle."

CORY WENT out back of the trucks with his Uncle John and they walked back and forth in the darkness.

"Is Mom going to die?" Cory asked, and in his mind it seemed a strange thing for him to say.

"Of course not. Don't talk like that."

"She looked—bad. So white."

"That's because she lost blood. She's got to have rest."

The doctor called them and they started back toward the train. He came to meet them. His manner was petulant.

"That woman has got to have shelter! You've got to get her up off the ground—into one of the atom-drives."

Cory looked at their own sorry truck with the warped floor. A cold shudder swept him.

"Nate Goodrow went to see," John Balleau said. "He's talking to some of the people. He'll be back soon."

Cory Balleau went back and sat down on the ground beside his mother. He took her hand and held it in his own. It was cold and he rubbed it gently, warming it. His mother, lay with her eyes closed, her face pointed straight upward toward the stars.

Cory sat there for a long time while the stars burned and from up and down the street came the sounds of people moving and laughing and talking and living.

He sat there for a long time and then he knew that his mother was dead.

He got stiffly to his feet and walked a little way down the street. He stopped and put out his hand and leaned against a truck.

There was a voice he could hear and he looked up and saw Nate Goodrow walking by in the gloom, going toward the Balleau truck. Another man was with him.

Nate Goodrow said, "I shouldn't have told them it was *marsplague,* I guess. They're touchy about havin' their trucks—"

The voice trailed off and was gone, but Cory knew. No trucks for his mother to die in. In this ghastly new world where men fought like animals and gouged out each other's eyes, there was no one who cared to give a woman the comfort of a dry, warm deathbed.

Cory Balleau, aged eleven, stood on the Martian prairie and sampled the taste of hatred.

When he returned to the truck a woman was there—a plump, pretty woman with a shawl over her head. She was scolding Nate Goodrow. "Why didn't you talk to me? Why didn't you tell me?"

Nate said, "I talked to your husband, ma'am."

The mother of the golden-haired girl bit her lip as she turned and saw Cory. She went to him and put her arms around him. "You poor boy! Poor lad!" Her sympathy was deep and genuine and the old Cory would have known and responded. The new Cory understood, but he could not respond.

He said, "Take your hands off of me!"

Startled, she looked into his eyes and saw the blaze of hatred. One so young—

"I said take your hands off me!" He turned from her and her arms dropped to her sides. She stared after him as he walked away.

"What an odd child. What a very odd child!"

CHAPTER TWO

JOHN BALLEAU had an eye for the soil and a love of growing things. In the years before the Third Atomic War, he had owned Willowrood, jointly with his brother, Robert Balleau, in the State of Mississippi. On Willowrood, the buildings were trim and neat; the family mansion gleamed white behind its massive pillars; the crops were the largest, by far, of any for miles around.

John and Robert Balleau were an ideal team. The fiery Robert maintained the social standard. He dashed about in fine racing cars, swept his wide-brimmed hat off to smiling ladies, and practiced the old arts of sword and pistol so full of ceremony and elegance. He married the most beautiful girl in all Mississippi as he was indeed expected to do and brought her home to Willowrood in a sleek jet from a European honeymoon. He sired one child, a son he named Cory, and was visibly disappointed when the boy, even at an early age, showed a leaning toward the gentler, more dreamy nature of his mother.

John, on the other hand, stayed in the background, and was quite content to give the stage to his brother. John preferred to live with the land. He was far more interested in the strength of a green stalk than in the burnish and temper of a sword blade. Over the sprained leg of a horse he was sure and gentle, but bending over the hand of a woman he acquired a clumsiness and redness of skin that ill became a gentleman.

As the war lumbered toward its outbreak, Robert Balleau was in the forefront of the flaming west-hemisphere vocalists. He flung defiance around the globe with fine gestures while John surveyed the fields in glum silence. The declaration of war found Robert at the head of a parajet regiment. He faced the future as a great adventure from which nothing but great reward could come. John accepted his captaincy without flourish and rode away wondering if the steel-dust mare could foal safely in his absence.

The Battle of Greenland, and elation swept the west. It would soon be over. But the east hurled its legions into the air and the war went on. During the first year, Robert died at the annihilation of the Second Lunar Platform. In the second year, sky raiders appeared and Faith Balleau stood in silence with Cory in her arms and watched the mansion flash into nothing. There was hunger and deep silent grief and time passing. The hordes of Gardis moving west unchecked. Surrender at Portland, and John Balleau came limping home. He stopped on the rise overlooking the broad acres and more of him died than had died in the war because now his one last hope had fled.

Willowrood was done. The Balleaus were penniless.

John Balleau put his hands to tools and worked a small strip of the land for vegetables, for immediate food, and a tiny spark of hope was revived. It would be a bad time stretching on ahead, but there *was* reconciliation. John Balleau had read the New Code. He had memorized passages from the Second Inspirational Address and he decided the wounds would be healed.

But with the New York Massacres, the spark of hope in the breast of John Balleau vanished.

HE DROPPED his tools and turned his eyes skyward. As always, he thought in terms of the land, the soil. There were acres on Mars to be had for the homesteading. He broached the subject to his sister-in-law, Faith. She shrugged. It made little difference—Mississippi, Luna, Venus, Mars. In truth, she had died with Robert Balleau.

They left Willowrood without a backward glance. They bought passage on a slow space-freighter at Panama and found—upon reaching Marsport—that others had also had the dream. They bought a dilapidated truck for three times its value and joined a guarded train for the southward trails.

After the crossing of the River—where Faith Balleau surrendered almost gratefully to the flame in her lungs— John dug a grave, after which he put the boy Cory on the seat of the truck and resumed what—to him—had become a sort of pilgrimage.

Day followed day and now it had become commonplace for a single truck or a small group of them to veer suddenly off at a tangent from the main train. A wave of a hand and these hardy seekers would fade into the vastness of the red prairie.

They've come home—each one of them knows that they've come home at last, Robert Balleau would say to himself upon these occasions, and as the crimson hills loomed in front of the train only to vanish rearward, he studied the landscape with a new intensity.

One day he called to a scout who was riding train-side, a young Terran named Nate Goodrow. "Where are we?"

Goodrow pulled in close, his eyes on the boy Cory, who rode on the seat beside his uncle; a boy who, upon the crossing of the river, seemed to have changed from an eleven year-old child to an eleven-year-old man. Cory had lost his childhood in a brief span of hours and no longer ran and played, nor did he allow his face to be the mirror of his emotion. He had acquired a dignity that his years denied and there was about him a gravity of bearing.

"Western edge of the Seven Canals." Nate Goodrow said. "Fine country. Rich land around here. How are you Cory?"

The boy turned his head. "I'm fine Mr. Goodrow."

"As one scout to another—why don't you call me Nate?"

Cory smiled briefly, and his reaction appeared to be one of mild amusement. "Thank you—Nate."

"Figuring on pulling off hereabouts. Mr. Balleau?"

"I like the look of it."

"I'll tell you something. There's a town up the line a piece. About ten miles. Peaceful natives. I've got a hunch there'll be quite a chunk of the train cut off there. I've heard some talk."

"Thank you—thank you very much."

With that John Balleau leaned on his wheel and swung out of line. A shout went up along the train. Hands were waved as John Balleau struck a forty five-degree angle and pulled away.

"I'll be hunting you up one of these days," Goodrow called.

The farewells were loud and cheerful and the hands and hats were waved with gusto. John Balleau turned and smiled and waved back.

But the boy Cory made no motions of acknowledgement. He stared straight ahead across the prairie. So far as his actions were concerned, the truck train did not exist.

John Balleau's instincts were unerring. They led him across the country straight to a spot where an eight-foot creek meandered into a swale and became a pond. There was lush grass here and cool yellow trees. The land sloped southward—gently rolling prairie-land that would respond to the love and care of a man like John Balleau.

He hit the brake and stopped beside the pond, got off the truck and picked up a handful of dirt. He let it dribble through his fingers. He said, "This is it, Cory boy. We're here."

Cory Balleau got down from the truck and took off his shoes. He stripped down and ran straight into the pond until it caught him around his lean hips. Then he pitched forward and sank to the soft bottom. The water felt good against his hot skin.

CHAPTER THREE

THE ANCIENT settlement of Ngania expanded a hundred-fold overnight. As the truck train wound in off the prairie, the thin sprinkling of natives blinked in wonder. A place with no ambitions and little energy, it found itself suddenly engulfed in the drive and action of a super-charged Terran horde.

Frank Bates was an excellent example of this new blood. He scanned the situation swiftly and what he saw was good. This country was rich and ripe and ready for the plow. In the not too distant future a freighter station would be established at Ngania and a flood of grain would pour into the space liners. The crying need would be for money, and Frank Bates had money. Money would be needed to build the country and the town. Lumber, farm implements, crop loans. The land was for the taking but that was only the beginning. The great common denominator was money.

The first important building to rise in Ngania was the imposing home of Frank Bates. The next building housed his Ngania Bank. The lumber was carted down from the polar forests in trucks and then there were more people who wanted homes and Frank Bates made arrangements with Terran banking connections and the money was forthcoming.

But there was a gross error in this picture and Frank Bates was comfortably aware of that error. It lay in the timing of the hopeful project.

The timing was wrong. Wheat and corn did not—like cattle—have legs. It could not be driven over the trails to the freighter station. The station must, of necessity, be at the back door of the grain fields in order to move the grain to market.

There was optimistic talk of course. The settlers were riding on a wave of enthusiasm and rumors flew thick and fast—rumors, but very few facts.

Frank Bates dreamed and planned, but he kept his dreams and plans to himself. He walked the streets of Ngania and had a smile and a handshake for all comers. And anyone who wished to discuss a loan against his land was cordially invited into the office.

At the end of two years, Frank Bates had quietly, and in the natural course of business, acquired four sections of land southwest of Ngania. In the drawer of his desk he had a map. When he was quite alone, with no chance of interruption, he would spread this map on his desk and study it with deep intent. The map was of a remarkably wide area of the surrounding country and, as time went on, Frank Bates blacked out more and more squares on the map. Black was his color of conquest. The blacked-out squares belonged to him and as he sat in his office, pencil in hand; he dreamed cocky little dreams of empire.

ONE DAY his eyes roved northeast on the map and he pursed his lips thoughtfully. He had been thinking of a place away from town—a spot upon which to build a country estate that would reflect his fast growing importance in the community. An ideal location for this would be on the land of John Balleau, a Terran who had come in with the first movement. On this land a meandering creek widened into a pond of pleasant proportions. There were trees there—a grove of yellow throngas. And trees were not too plentiful in this prairie.

However, this John Balleau had not borrowed any money from the Ngania Bank. He was a wary customer, this Terran. With the tools he brought, he had pushed his cultivation out gradually from the small house he'd built with his own wood. He refused to get over-extended, shunned obligation, and ignored rumors of the coming station. He preferred to wait until he saw the ships on the horizon.

The months and the seasons passed and the years became four. The freighters did not come, and Frank Bates continued blacking out sections of his map. Settlers continued to pack up their trucks and move onward off land no longer theirs.

Strangely enough, they did not blame Frank Bates. The man had a way of ingratiating himself. He had a knack of appearing to be an effect rather than a cause. He shunted the curses off on the Terran capitalists and even sped travelers on their way with a few cash credits to get them comfortably on the move.

He was still the genial greeter on the streets of Ngania, but fewer and fewer settlers were received in his private office.

And he was content with his land, his dreams and his plans. If he was growing a trifle harder, a little more rapacious, somewhat more openly arrogant, no one really noticed it.

His wife, Myra, a plump, pleasant woman with no great ambitions, served as an excellent front. She was a sincere and gracious hostess, a figure in the social life of the town. Also, she was not a difficult woman for her husband to handle.

His daughter was a golden-haired beauty of whom he was very proud. With the passing of four more years, she had turned eighteen and, to her father's satisfaction, had remained emotionally unentangled. With her, Frank Bates had been more direct and open in his relations. She was important to him. She was not going to be wasted upon any cow-eyed local youth. She would eventually meet and marry New York class, Terran breeding of course, with limitless money.

In his own way he gave her to understand this and he was satisfied with the docility with which she accepted her destiny. He would have liked her to be a bit more of a snob. He regretted that she had the common touch so apparent in her mother, but he was aware of the fire lying close under her calm exterior and attributed that to his own blood running through her veins.

There were times when he thought he sensed a cunning in her, an essence of the inner fire that disquieted him. At times, he had a feeling that, behind her clear blue eyes, she was laughing at him. But this, he knew of course, was only his imagination.

Kay Bates was the greatest satisfaction of his life.

CHAPTER FOUR

KAY BATES had a petite three-horned *goff* and she spent a great deal of time in the saddle. She had expensive Terran riding clothes—jodhpurs clinging to her slim legs to bulge out at the thigh; black boots and vivid shirtwaists and trim jackets. The clothes gave her complete freedom and she wore them as she wore her lush body—with unassuming grace.

Upon this day—as upon other days—she rode directly north from Ngania until she came to Bland Creek. Then, well out of sight of the town, she veered eastward, following the bends of the creek, skirting the thronga patches, until she was upon the land of John Balleau.

As she traveled, a definite transformation came over her. Her eyes brightened and the breathing movement of her bosom became deeper and more hurried. She leaned forward on the *goff* and was impatient with any inclination of the animal to dally by the way. Her cheeks were brightly flushed and, at times, her smooth brown hands almost trembled.

At one turn in the creek, sheltered by a thick growth of thronga, the *goff* snorted, ears turned sharply forward. The animal tossed its alert head and Kay saw the rump and switching tail of another *goff* cropping red grass in the swale beyond. Then the sounds of splashing water and Kay was off the sorrel and creeping swiftly through the willows. She ran toward the creek and the feeling within her was warm and delicious. She pushed head and shoulders out of concealment into a grassed-over glade.

Here the creek—at one of its many bends—went to twice its normal width and swirled in a pocket of respectable depth. The splashing sounds had been coming from there.

Kay stepped into full view and looked down at the slim brown body that was rolling and twisting and disporting in the water. A turning motion, and the entire left side of this body was visible for a moment above the water line. Then a quick turn to its back to do a complete forward flip, slide into the depths and leave only the heels in sight. Now the head came up—thick brown curls flinging water like a seal—a brown fare and blue eyes opening.

Kay's laugh was clear and happy.

"Cory!"

Cory Balleau was nineteen now and he had received the physical heritage of his father. The slim perfection of body, from the shoulders down, was that of Robert Balleau. The shoulders themselves were broader and stronger, but despite hard work, they would never bulge with muscle. The classic line was almost intact.

The face, now flushed deep red, was also of the sensitive, classic mold.

"How long have you been there?" he gasped.

Her lie was tossed back gaily, "A long time. I was in the willows, peeking. I'm a shameless hussy."

"That's the truth! You turn around and get yourself away from here."

She made motions against the buttons of her blouse. "I'm coming in."

"You're not! I'll—I'll drown you. Get back in the throngas!"

"I'm tired of peeking. I want to swim."

She teased him with every fiber of her mind and body—with her eyes and her lips and the tilt of her breast and the slant of her hips and legs. Something inside her was wildly exultant at his embarrassment.

"Love me?" she asked coyly.

"No! You Martian trollop!"

IT IS SAID that there is always one man before whom each woman is shameless. This may or may not be true, but Kay Bates, who was the despair of every swain in Ngania, whose lips, so far as they were concerned, were used only for laughing, listened to this hurled insult and grinned, gamin-like.

"Shall I dance for you?"

"You can get away from here for me!"

"Come on out."

"I won't come out."

She dropped cross-legged to the ground. "I can wait. You stay there and pretty soon the sun will go away. Then you'll get blue and your teeth will chatter. Hadn't you better come out now while it's warm?"

"All right. If that's how you want it." He started grimly toward the bank. But it was only a bluff and he was never to find out whether it would have scared her away. He had a feeling that it wouldn't and he stopped belly deep in the water.

"Please!"

Her gayety dropped from her and there was something in her eyes; something of a wordless question, as though her eyes were saying: Can't you *understand* this?

She said, "Cory…" And there was a pleading in her voice. Then she said, "All right. Hurry and get dressed."

She turned and stepped over his clothing, snatched up his shirt and disappeared through the throngas.

Soon he followed, to find her stretched full length in the grass of the swale where the *goffs* were cropping through their bits. She had folded his shirt into a pillow that was almost covered by her golden hair.

"Give it here," Cory demanded.

She looked at his upper body, tanned to a deep flawless brown, up into his eyes. She was strangely quiet.

He dropped, cross-legged beside her. A twist and her head was in the pocket formed by his knees, her face turned upward to his.

His hand moved over and his fingers clenched and kneaded in the strands of her hair. "Why are you...?"

"Why am I what?"

"Well—like you are?"

A shadow of the gamin grin but a wistfulness underneath. "Don't you like me this way?"

"I—don't know."

"Can't you find out?"

"This is no good. Sneaking around like this."

"I'm not sneaking. I just ride out. I don't try to stop anyone from following me."

She knew that this was not true, that she was very careful to avoid pursuit. And she knew why. This was, of course, against her father's will, and he would terminate it swiftly if he knew. It is doubtful that she would have deceived him concerning any other phase of her life. Aside from this passionate attachment, she was an open book to him or anyone else because it was not her nature to be otherwise. However, she was a girl who had found the one male who could stir the woman-fires within her. Beside Cory Balleau, all the youths she had ever met seemed shallow, ungainly lumps of clay. She was possessed of a passion that could be set off only by something this youth possessed.

THE FEELING he engendered within her had a fierce quality about it that—so far as she was concerned—went deeper than any code of honesty. The rules whereby she had been taught to live had nothing to do with her love for Cory Balleau.

Thus her deceit in defending this love was complete and crafty. And in keeping it under cover, she did not reveal any weakness or any craven tinge of spirit, but rather a sure knowledge that her father was stronger than she was. In any battle over this passion of hers, her father would win. This she knew.

"Isn't it pretty odd that no one ever has followed you?"

She reached up and caught his hands and drew them down to her breast. Her eyes were closed.

"Lets not talk."

"We've got to talk."

"Why?"

"Because—because we've got to come to an understanding. You've got—to stay away from here."

"I'm not going to stay away."

She sighed with contentment and snuggled her head deeper into his lap. His words did not upset her. She knew her weaknesses and she knew her strength. She was well aware of the fact that she had not stirred this youth as he stirred her. But also, she knew that, eventually, she would.

And, in the meantime, he would not drive her away. It was only in connection with this sure knowledge that she ever gave any thought to her body. It was holding him, whether he knew it or not, and she was fiercely thankful that she had a beautiful body, slim legs and smooth hips and a strong sexual lure. In these moments she sometimes thought: *Suppose I was ugly and lumpy and had nothing to attract him—nothing to hold him until I can make him feel the love I feel. I think I'd die.*

If the time ever comes when I can't see him and feel him and look forward to someday having him completely, I know I'll die—

I know that—

CORY BALLEAU'S feelings, relative to Kay Bates, were vague, blurred of outline and somewhat troublesome to the youth. He felt an attraction to the lips and the body that were wantonly held out to him, but there was a barrier within him that stood between; a barrier he could not surmount.

Nor did he entirely understand what this block was—a dozen generations of genteel breeding coupled with a nature that was a trifle cold—that did not inflame easily. The sexual pull of Kay Bates was apparent to Cory Balleau; it was an attraction but not an all-powerful magnet. There was need for more in a woman, so far as Cory was concerned. A deeper response had to be engendered within himself and that response was not there.

In truth, the boy was afraid of life. He seldom left the homestead acres his uncle had acquired northeast of Ngania. He worked the land and swam in the creek and took the seasons as they came and was content if not happy.

He was sure that he wanted no more than this. In the town itself, when he went there with his uncle, he was distinctly ill at ease. Back in his sensitive mind were old images—old and hazed over by time, but none-the-less potent in his subconscious mind. He felt that the world was a grim conscienceless hodgepodge of brutal beings without feeling for each other. Greed and cruelty lay within the hearts of everyone. Any indication to the contrary was mere insincerity that lay as a thin coating over their true natures. He had seen stark evidence of this cruelty, and, except in his now-dead mother, in his uncle, and in Kay Bates, he never seen any sign of the goodness of man.

As a matter of fact, he sensed a streak of cruelty in Kay herself, and he felt that possibly her efforts to get what she wanted—if crossed—would border on cruelty.

Riding slowly homeward, Cory Balleau wondered uneasily about Kay Bates. What held him back from the girl? He had the feeling that, through stubbornness or sheer stupidity, he was eschewing something of great delight. The rich manhood in his body, held in check behind the deeply bred obstructions, was sullen and complaining.

Then, as the house and outbuildings came in sight, Cory heeled his *goff* and forgot about Kay Bates. There was a big black *goff* in the yard and the boy was suddenly happy.

He hurtled across the back field, yelling at the top of his lungs, "Nate! Nate Goodrow! You old son-of-a-son-of-a-son-of-a-son! Nate!"

A gangling form appeared from the back door of the house as Cory cleared the back fence, skidded from his *goff* and pelted across the footbridge at the narrow end of the pond.

Nate Goodrow had changed little in eight years. And, to the youth, he had changed none at all because his periodic visits were frequent enough to make any aging imperceptible. He was still steel under purple leather, and the hand he wrapped around that of Cory Balleau had the grip of a vise.

"Ambling back down south," he drawled. "Stopped off of course. Wanted to see if you still fit your pants."

"You're staying a while, aren't you? Sure you are! You've got to tell me about your trip. How far did you get into the north forest country?"

CHAPTER FIVE

JOHN BALLEAU followed the visitor from the house. "Take it easy, Cory. He just got here. And by the way, where have you been? We're waiting supper."

"I was swimming," Cory replied, his eyes still on Nate Goodrow.

His uncle smiled. He enjoyed seeing the sparkle in Cory's eyes and the vitality bubbling to the surface. The boy was too quiet. He existed too much within himself. He seemed to brood a lot and that worried John Balleau.

The lack of a mother had a great deal to do with it, of course. John Balleau had done his best, but no man could take the place of a boy's mother.

It had been a terrific shock to Cory, back there on the Marsport River when his mother had died. He'd never been away from his mother for a single day up to that time.

At the river, he had stiffened overnight and jumped the years of childhood in a matter of hours. To John Balleau, his shyness and tendency to seek solitude appeared to stem from that time. He didn't care to visit Ngania alone or in company with the elder Balleau. Cory should know others of his own age, his uncle believed. He should have contact with young women. It bothered John Balleau that Cory was not on speaking terms with a single young Terran woman in Ngania or the surrounding country.

"The weather hit us up in the forest country," Nate Goodrow was saying. "The train holed up south of the fringe and I meandered back. Came down through the Sweet Water. Guess I got a hankering for the south. Got me a piece of land near the Red Canal and I'm going to settle down."

John Balleau smiled as he pushed his chair back from the table and lit his pipe. "How long do you think you'll be able to sit tight? You weren't made for sitting. I figure you'll be coming north again soon and that maybe you'll take Cory on your next trip."

"Say, now that wouldn't be a bad idea. How about it, son?"

Cory smiled briefly. "Uncle John couldn't get along without me here. He'd bog down in a week."

"How do things look for you?"

"Good—good," Balleau said. "The air-freight's coming at last. This country will boom now. It looks as though we've been able to wait it out."

Goodrow sobered. "That's fine. Too bad a lot of those other first settlers couldn't hang on."

Later, stretched on the lawn John Balleau had built down to a pleasant curve in the pond, Nate Goodrow was taking his ease. He watched Cory skidding flat stones across the water.

"You've never had any itch to see the country at all, have you, son?"

Cory dropped to the soft sod beside his friend; "I guess not. I don't know. It's pretty nice here. I guess I don't care much how anybody else lives.'"

"From what I hear, you don't take after your daddy. He cut himself quite a swath back on Terra."

"I guess he did all right."

CORY HAD only fleeting memories of his father. A kind, mercurial man who was never in one spot for any great length of time. He always thought of the past in terms of his mother, and the bittersweet memories invariably left him depressed.

"I doubt if I'll be coming north again, son. Getting kind of old and stiff in the bones. I want you to remember the name, Candalla. Nice little town. Nice country. Want you to remember that name and swing down to see me sometime. You'll want to move around before long. It isn't natural for a boy to cling to one spot all his life."

Cory rolled over and looked at the sky; "How many men have you killed, Nate?"

"Eh?"

"I said—how many men have you killed in your time?"

The scout was a trifle surprised at the abruptness of the query; "Counting Martians you mean?"

"I suppose so. Counting all of them." Cory reached over and drew the Gort knife from its sheath on Nate's thigh. The shining blade threw back the rays of the lowering sun and was thus tinged with a red hue. There was a worn line around Nate Goodrow's waist, spilling down to a large shiny spot on his right thigh. The pellet belt and the black pyro-gun were in on the living room table.

"Don't rightly know now, son. It's pretty hard to stay peaceable and tramp over the country like I do in these times."

Cory ran the tip of his finger along the edge of the knife.

"I keep it right sharp," Nate said. "Use it to shave with quite a little."

Cory held out the knife. "Hit something with it—the way you used to when I was a kid."

Nate took the knife by its blade-tip, held it between the first sections of his right thumb and first finger. His wrist flopped limply as he looked around seeking a target.

"That fly," Cory said.

The fly was on a post some twenty feet away. Nate raised his arm and there was a movement of blurred leather. The knife became a glimmering arc in the air.

"Missed," Nate said.

The knife quivered and was still, its blade buried an inch in the post. The fly was not in sight. Nate got to his feet and stretched his long arms. "Who owns all the land that was homesteaded by the pilgrims in the first train—the ones that couldn't hold out?"

"The bank I guess—most of it. A man named Bates owns the bank so I guess he owns most of the land."

"It'll payoff right handsome now the ships are coming through."

CHAPTER SIX

FRANK BATES' dream of Martian empire was growing apace. As his holdings increased so did his sense of sureness and his confidence in himself. Also, his attitude toward right and wrong took on a new and darker hue and his sense of justice became covered over with the tarnish of avarice.

After all, it was purely a matter of the survival of the fittest. Any feeling of brotherhood he had ever had for pilgrims struggling and blundering toward independence had turned to pity and then—as his land holdings expanded—had become impersonal contempt. The land should not be sliced up into tittle garden patches, he opined. He subscribed to the economic principle of monopoly as a convenient way of justifying himself as the core of that monopoly.

Seated at his desk, with his map before him, he smiled in satisfaction at the tremendous black area southwest of Ngania. He had plans for that land, and upon this day, one of those plans had been consummated. There was a *goff* waiting outside the bank. Bates the left his office, mounted the animal, and rode southwest.

The cattle had been there since dawn—scrawny bone-bags, the scum of a dozen Terran herds assembled. Three hundred wrecks. A man, idling by the herd, turned his *goff* and came to meet Bates as the latter approached.

The man was a great shaggy hulk of bone and muscle. He dwarfed the *goff* he rode and had a belligerent tilt to his head and shoulders. Red dust was thick on his luxuriant whiskers.

"Hello, Frake," Bates said.

"All safe," the man returned. "Only, ten died on the freighter."

"Your man was in town early this morning. I got out as soon as I could."

Frake had no comment. He swung his great head left and right—eyes squinting. "I'm quite a cattleman."

"How did the trip go?"

Frake replied, "We came slow—cost less on the slow freighters—and it wasn't as bad as I thought it'd be. It was the start that stuck in my craw."

"How so?"

Frake scowled. "Did you ever walk up to a Terran cattleman and say: 'Got any half-dead vulture bait for sale, mister? I'm looking for any old bags of bones that can stand without being propped up. I'm going to ship them to Mars!' Did you ever walk up to a cattleman and say that?"

Bates smiled faintly. "No I never did."

"They're laughing all over West America. They'll spend the next ten years wondering what I wanted of this worm-eaten mess."

"Let them wonder," Bates said. "They were cheap and they'll serve the purpose much better than valuable stock."

"I hold title—is that it?" Frake asked.

"Of course. That's the most important angle. I'm renting you grazing land."

"We didn't go into the details about men," Frake said.

"You'll need them, of course."

"By the way, mister," Frake said. "What's the law around here?"

"In a word—I am. We have a town marshal...man named Dalton. You'll deal with him through me if the need for dealing should ever arise."

"I want to keep two of the boys with me. The other three are heading back to Terra. With Mel Dorken and Tip Snead I think I can get along for a while."

Bates extended a canvas bag. "A thousand credits a month for you and three hundred for your men. When the job's finished we'll discuss a bonus."

Frake took the bag and Bates said, "That's gold. Any money transactions will always be in cash. Nothing on paper. No receipts."

"When do we start operating?" Frake asked.

BATES SWUNG suddenly from his saddle, bent backwards and stood rubbing the small of his back. "I'll let you know. I'll tell you the time and the place and exactly what to do." He glanced sharply at Frake. "It's understood without question that I'm boss. You do as I say, when I say."

Bates would have been surprised to know how little men of Frake's ilk cared about bosses. Frake grinned and raised his hand and tipped it in what might have been a mock salute.

"Right—boss."

"This wouldn't have been necessary if they'd held the freighter station off another year, I'd have gotten what I wanted through ordinary legal procedure then. But it's coming and so my hand is being forced. You'll get orders very soon."

Frake said nothing, and Bates went on, saying, "These men Dorken and Snead—are they trustworthy?"

Frake grinned now. "That's a hell of a word to use in the kind of business you're going into."

Bates flushed. "All right. I'll leave the men to you. But let me know before you take on any more."

Frake tossed the moneybag into the air. He caught it in a palm into which it disappeared completely. "Where do we bunk?"

"You'd better make your headquarters at the old Croft place, about six miles due east of here. It's been abandoned for some time but the building is in fair condition."

Bates remounted and looked out toward the herd. His lips twisted in amusement. "I hope they'll live long enough to serve our purpose," he said.

Frake grinned back.

Bates glanced back at Frake, raised his hand and put heels to his mount.

As he moved off across the prairie, the grin slid from Frake's face. He sat staring thoughtfully after the retreating figure. He was even now wondering how this affair would terminate. There was always an ending. These things could never be plotted through in advance. They always took unexpected turns. Frake's talent lay in his ability to take good care of himself under any and all circumstances.

"That's the way it sits," he was telling two men over the fire that evening. "I only know part of what Bates has got up his sleeve. Maybe it's good and maybe it isn't but if things start flying to pieces, there's no reason why we shouldn't stick around with a basket."

Tip Snead shrugged. "Why not?"

There was a great deal of a snake about this man. He had the look of a snake in the flatness of his face; the expression of a snake in the cold opaqueness of his eyes;

and the treachery of a snake in the way he could slide a knife from his sleeve and hurl it into a man's back.

"Why not?" Snead said matter-of-factly. "What have we got to lose?"

The third man was of Frake's cut—a mountain with a beard. He was nothing much more than a skinful of cruelty walking around on two legs. There were no acts of viciousness, sadism, or lust in the whole gamut that Mel Dorken had not committed. And his vice wasn't merely limited to human kind. There was a trick with cats. You tied the tails of two Toms together and threw them over a clothesline. A no more primitive nor vicious combat could be arranged; one to sicken the stomachs of even hardened men. Mel Dorken liked to find two trusting cats. There were things that could be done, with fire, to dogs. Dorken knew of these things.

With women—

Mel Dorken lived only to satisfy his senses. The physical appetites were paramount. Nothing beyond them mattered.

"Count me in," he said, lazily. "You ride herd tonight, Tip. I'm tired."

"Let them drift," Frake said. "We'll all sleep."

"COULDN'T LET the land stand idle," Frank Bates told an inquirer in Ngania, "so I rented it out as grazing land. Just temporary of course."

"I was wondering," the inquirer replied. "Seemed odd to bring in cattle at this stage of the game—with the road coming through the farmer's fight is won."

"It's going to be a great country," Bates said. "If any of the boys want to sell out, tell them to see me. I'll back this country with my last credit."

"I guess most of them will hang on now. In fact there'll probably be some buyers nosing around—"

"Yes sir! I believe in this country." Frank Bates gave the man a hearty handshake and went into his bank.

CHAPTER SEVEN

IN LATE afternoon of the following Saturday, John Balleau pulled up in front of the largest general store in Ngania—Galpin's Complete Supply. He jumped from the light truck and glanced back to where Cory still remained on the seat.

"I've got some business at the bank and I'll have to hurry to catch Frank Bates."

"How long will you be?"

"Not more than an hour. Meet me in the Golden King and we'll have a drink before we go home."

Cory didn't care much for liquor, but it made little difference where he killed the time. He nodded and got down from the wagon.

John Balleau hurried down the street toward the most imposing building in Ngania. He went inside; a shirt-sleeved clerk looked out from behind a grill.

"Is Mr. Bates in?" Balleau asked.

The clerk turned away without answering and went through a door to the left. He hesitated in the doorway.

"Tell him John Balleau is calling."

The words carried and Frank Bates appeared immediately at the door. His smile was cordial. "Come in. Come in. A pleasure to see you, Sir."

He stepped back and John Balleau went into the small office. The clerk went back to his glass.

Bates indicated a chair beside his desk, sat down, and leaned back expansively in his plastic-back swivel.

"I dropped in to talk about the railroad," Balleau said. "I thought you might have some late information."

Frank Bates laughed. "I haven't got any more than anyone else, but the line's coming through. It will be a two-station mile spur northwest from the Second Canal System. The first freighter will pull into Ngania in less than three Marsmonths."

Balleau nodded. "It will be a great thing for the section. Looks as though a man could borrow crop credits now with a fair degree of safety."

"I'm glad to hear you say that," Bates returned, heartily. "You showed rare judgment in holding off. Too bad others didn't follow your example."

"Some of them probably acted upon bad advice."

Bates shrugged. "No doubt. We run a bank, though, and you can't refuse people loans if they have the security."

"What would you say my place would stand in the way of a loan?"

"There won't be any trouble on that score. You've got the best set of buildings for miles around. You've got a well-located place and good land. How much do you have in mind?"

"I thought I'd buy a cultivator-unit and a seeder. We'll really need them now. And throw up a couple of granaries, so we'll be ready. About two thousand?"

"With pleasure..." Bates came erect and started for the door. "I'll get the papers ready for you. Won't be a minute. We may as well finish it up now."

He opened the outer door and turned back. "Shall we make it twelve Marsmonths? Does that suit you?"

John Balleau hesitated. "I'd like to play entirely safe. How about eighteen?"

"Of course. We're here to serve. Eighteen it is."

HE WENT into the bank proper and John Balleau leaned back in his chair. He wasn't as confident as he would have like to be but it seemed that he had no choice. The money was needed in order to raise a crop. The time had come to extend himself. Nonetheless, he shrank from the prospect.

Bates returned with a sheaf of papers. He laid them on the desk and stood over John Balleau.

"Here it is," he said. "A regular eighteen-month form—there in the print." He reached over and picked up a pen from the desk. "Six percent straight. You sign in three places."

He checked off the signature lines and then straightened up, still holding the pen. "By the way—do you want any cash now—today?"

"A couple of hundred would be convenient."

"Fine—fine. I wonder if you'd just step out to the grill and sign for it? Fred will give it to you right away. It's closing time and he likes to get out."

John Balleau went into the banking room and returned, a few minutes later, with a handful of green credits. He folded it carefully and put it into his pocket.

"Your John Henry three times and we're all set," Bates smiled.

Balleau sat down and affixed the necessary signatures. He leaned back with a sigh as Bates called, "Henry, come here and witness this, will you? It won't take a second."

The clerk, a pale little oldster, came into the office. He signed mutely in the proper spaces, and scuttled out.

Bates picked up one of the sheets and folded it three times. "Your copy," he said, "and it's been a pleasure."

John Balleau got up from his chair, folded the sheet again and put it in with the money. "You're very accommodating. I appreciate it."

"Any time," Frank Bates said, and he slapped John Balleau's shoulder cordially as he let him out the front door.

CORY BALLEAU wandered aimlessly up the street after he had finished his business at Carter's. He stood for some time in front of Sam Helger's—Gunsmith, surveying the stock in the small window. There were three pyro-guns—hand weapons—heavy and competent; a para-rifle, which he knew nothing about, and an atom cutter—a slim-looking weapon with a long barrel.

At home there were two pyro-guns and a para-rifle. The rifle had never been out of his uncle's room so far as the youth knew. Cory had little interest in guns. A sprinkling of men went armed in the town, but few of the farmers ever wore guns.

Cory wandered on and walked in under the swinging wooden sign of the Golden King. It was dim and cool in there and a pleasant smell hit his nostrils. He stepped up to the bar and ordered tanza. It came in an immense cup and as he lifted it to his lips, the barkeep wiped the bar in front of him.

A card game was going on at a round table rearward of the long room. There were five men—three Terrans and two Martians—participating. Cory picked up his cup and wandered back. Only one of the players bore any resemblance to a gambler. He was a pale-faced man with a pair of expressionless eyes and a cold cigarette hanging loosely from his lips. He looked up and said, "Sit in, son? Open game—anybody can win."

Cory shook his head and the gambler accepted the deck from his right, shuffled with a few lightning movements, and pushed the deck back for a cut.

The door up front swung open and the dealer looked up, continuing to deal. Three men strode into the drinking room. Immediately the dealer looked less bored.

The three men stopped at the bar and were given a bottle from which each had several drinks. Then, wiping the backs of hairy hands across their mouths, they moved back toward the poker table.

The dealer smiled. "Glad to see you back, Mr. Frake."

The man addressed as Frake sat down at the table. His chair creaked under him. "Meet a couple of friends o' mine. Boys with credits and an itch in their fingers. Tip Snead, and Mel Dorken. I want you to treat 'em right when they come in here."

The dealer's smile was like a sheet of thin tissue paper over his face. "We always aim to do that, Mr. Frake. It's five-card stud."

Cory Balleau was in the grip of a cold chill. He turned from the table and walked back to the bar with slow, careful steps. He set his cup down, half-full and stared into the wavy mirror behind the bar. He saw a pale face staring back at him. Then the door opened and John Balleau was standing beside him.

The older man glanced at Cory and turned to face the mirror. But he turned back suddenly; "What's the matter, Cory? Are you all right?"

"I'm all right."

"Never saw you that pale before.

What are you drinking?"

"Just tanza."

CORY GRIPPED his schooner, trying to analyze and quell the cold shock within his body.

"Let's get out of here," he said.

John Balleau had a shot glass full of whisky raised to his lips. He tossed off the liquor and set the glass down. "Of course."

Out in the street, walking toward the wagon, Cory felt better. "Those three men—they came in just before you did. There at the poker table. Did you see them?"

"I saw them go in. I understand they rented some grazing land from Frank Bates. Why?"

"I was just wondering."

"Did they set you off some way?"

"No."

The two climbed into the truck and started home. John Balleau made no further inquiries. They rode in silence.

But there was a question in the mind of Cory Balleau: Why did I feel like that? And how did I know him—that man they called Mel Dorken? Just one look at his face and it was as if I'd seen him only yesterday. Nothing but eyes and nose and a beard—yet I knew him and I'd know him fifty years from now.

The way he held his thumbs out stiff on the table. He held them the same way after that fight back there on the Marsport River.

When he sat on that man and gouged his eyes out.

It was difficult to stir desire in Mel Dorken. The black cesspool of his mind had been satiated to the point that women had become more of a habit to him than an urge. He had practiced all the forms of debasement that the mind of man could imagine and there were none to ignite the smoldering ashes within him.

All the things that the mind of man could invent—Mel Dorken had done, and now a woman had to generate a terrific natural voltage in order to stir him.

But, riding one afternoon, north of Ngania, Mel Dorken felt the old, dimly remembered eruptions surging through his veins.

The girl was young—not more than twenty—and slimly arrogant in her carriage and in the freshness of her youth. Yellow hair cascaded down her shoulders.

Dorken had been riding at an angle with her course of travel, gradually narrowing the gap between them. As he came closer the surging within him increased until he felt his heart pounding inside him with a thunder that beat in his ears.

The girl was riding a spirited *goff* and she rode with uncertainty but she did not change her course. At the point of the angle formed by their trails, Mel Dorken came to a dead halt and stared in utter silence. The girl kept moving. She passed a point some ten yards ahead of Dorken and her eyes were on him, wide and unblinking, until she was well beyond the intersection. Then she straightened around and cut the *goff* with her quirt. The animal leaped forward as though fired from a gun, and girl and mount disappeared over a swell to the north.

Dorken did not move for five minutes. He stared after the girl and the light in his eyes was as unholy as a fiend saying Black Mass in the depths of some pit.

Kay Bates lay on the soft grass, her head on Cory Balleau's shoulder. She was unusually quiet, her blue eyes troubled.

Cory Balleau said, "Something bothering you?"

"I'm not sure—whether it ought to bother me or not."

"Tell me."

"As I was coming north, I crossed trails with a man—a stranger. I'd never seen him before."

"What did he do?"

"Nothing."

"Did he say something?"

"No—but—"

He tilted her face into line with his own. "But what? I never saw you short of words before."

"It was the way he looked at me. He was an immense, bushy brute and he looked at me as though he was—well—*undressing* me. I sort of burned clear down to my heels. It scared me."

He surveyed her face with mock criticism and then grinned. "Like this?" and he opened his eyes wide and ran the tip of his tongue along his lips.

"No, silly—it was—"

"There's no law against men looking at girls. I'd think you'd be used to it by now."

She shuddered slightly. "I'd never get used to that kind of a look…" She turned in a quarter-roll and put her face close to his. "…unless it was from you. Why don't you look at me that way?"

He lay back and looked up into the sky and laughed.

MEL DORKEN made his meandering way back to his headquarters. He took down the corral bars, lifted the saddle from his mount, and slipped its bridle. The *goff* kicked its heels and danced away, running in a tight circle before it went down into the dust and rubbed its hide against the ground.

Dorken threw his saddle over the corral rack and walked slowly toward the house. Inside Tip Snead was cooking supper. Frake was lounging at the kitchen table cleaning a para-rifle.

"You been sightseeing?" Snead asked.

"I saw me a sight. What a sight!"

Dorken threw his hat into a corner. He turned a chair around and sat down, leaning his arms against its back.

Frake looked at Snead. "I'd say he was talking about a woman."

"I'd say you was right," Snead answered. He flipped the bacon into the air and there was a cloud of acrid smoke from the burning grease.

"There's a yellow-top girl riding around the country," Dorken said. "About twenty, maybe, and she burns a man to a crisp just lookin' at her. Any idea who she belongs to?"

"Why?" Snead asked. "You want to go out and kill him?"

Frake scowled and said, "There'll be no killing there. I saw her in town the other day. She belongs to the man we work for—she's Bates' daughter."

Snead grinned. "Now isn't that just luck? To get the gal you want, you have to kill the bird that's got the golden eggs you want. Why is it always that way? The good things always tied together in a knot you can't unravel?"

Dorken said nothing. He had a quiet, almost vacant look on his face.

Frake eyed him sharply; "Whatever you're thinking is no good—understand that! We're not messing up this deal over a yellow-haired skirt. Keep your needs in check until they don't get in the way of important things. Women come every day, but a Bates drops around once in a lifetime."

"Maybe you're right," Dorken said.

He thought: *I've got to have that girl.* Come deals or hell or earthquake I've got to feel that yellow hair in my hands. When you want a certain woman the only thing that will stop the itching inside is to get that woman. Not anything in skirts, but *that* woman. That one.

"Pull up," Snead said. He dumped the contents of the frying pan onto a platter and set the platter on the table. The meal was ready.

FOR FIVE minutes there was an uninterrupted champing of hairy jaws as the men bolted the food. The platters cleaned, Dorken sat back and lit a cigarette.

"What's Bates waiting for?" Dorken asked. "I thought he had a lot of big plans. What the hell are they anyway?"

"He has got plans," Frake said. "We're going to fill in some squares in his checkerboard for him."

"Talk sense," Snead said.

"There's some land around here he wants, to make his holdings solid. A few of the nesters have held on too long and with the freight head coming, Bates has got to make a move."

"Like what?"

"Like our cattle drifting. Tonight, after dark we start. There's some four-inch corn shoots on a land over east. The herd drifts in and grazes that corn. By morning there won't be much left."

"It's a long way between tromping corn and taking over land."

"Not if you've got a plaster on the land that the corn's supposed to pay off."

Dorken was silent, staring at his cigarette.

"Bates takes the land when the mortgage comes due," Frake went on. "They're not his cattle that wrecked the crop. He's in the clear."

"So the squatter comes after us," Snead said.

Frake grinned. "So he does. And what have we got? A damn bone yard he'd have to sue to get and wouldn't be worth anything after he got it." Frake grinned. "You afraid of being sued, Tip?"

The little knife artist was far from satisfied.

"Sounds like penny-ante stuff to me. How much territory can three hundred head cover?"

"It isn't so much what they cover as where it's located. This little raid tonight will get Bates two hundred acres. The corn's all this nester's got and he won't be able to plant another stand this year. He ain't got the seed or the time. We pull three or four like that before we're smoked out and Bates has got a nice lump of land."

"Maybe," Tip said.

"And later, there may be some fires. You never can tell."

Dorken leaned forward. "All right. So Bates gets his land. What have we got?"

Frake grinned. "We've got Bates."

"That's right," Snead said.

But Dorken scarcely heard, so quickly had his mind wandered. He was thinking of a head of shining yellow hair.

He had to have that woman.

CHAPTER EIGHT

EVERYTHING was gone. The land he'd cultivated and worked and seeded so carefully—the soft warm land—was torn and defiled by deep pockmarks. Cattle had been here and now all the precious stems had vanished into the bellies of the cattle. Effort—security—nothing left.

The sight was like a physical blow to the pit of the man's stomach. He stood motionless. His arms hung limp, his gnarled hands clenched into fists. His throat worked but no sounds came forth.

He turned and moved away from the field, back toward his barn and corral. A slow stiff walk at first, then increasing to a fast walk—faster until he was running and his breathing was in audible sobs.

At the corral he got a bridle and put it over the head of a sorry-looking *goff*. He led the animal out through the gate and then the man's wife came toward him across the back yard.

"What's the matter, Sam? Where are you going? Why've you been running? What's the matter?"

The man paid no heed. He forked the bare back of the *goff* and dug his heels into its flanks.

The man's breath continued in rasping sobs as he belabored the animal—beat his heels against its sides as it struggled to please him. The sweat on its flanks turned to lather. Foam flecked its mouth.

"All gone," the man kept muttering. "Wiped out! All gone!"

When the *goff* finally made Ngania, the lather was thick and the animal was staggering. The man slid to the ground; left the *goff* in the middle of the street in front of the office of Henry Dalton, marshal of Ngania. The office was housed in a small building that had been a gift to the town from Frank Bates. The front door was open.

Henry Dalton did not take his spurred boot off his desk as the man entered the office. Dalton, a wispy oldster with a white goatee serving as an extension of a weak chin, looked up and said, "Sam Bendorf... What's the trouble? You act like a man with his britches full of ants."

"My corn's all gone! It's been chewed off and tramped into the ground by cattle! I'm wiped out!"

"Are you sure you're all right, Sam? There aren't any cattle in these parts. You're going crazy, man."

"I seen the tracks with my own eyes. Cattle it was. A big herd."

HENRY DALTON'S face took on a calculating look. He tugged at his goatee. "Say now—guess maybe there are some beeves in the neighborhood. I heard a rumor that Frank Bates let out some of his land for grazing—rented to a Terra man."

"It was their cattle then that done it and I want justice. I want that feller locked up and made to pay!"

Dalton got slowly to his feet. "Now, Sam. You'd better simmer down a little. That isn't the way the law works and you know it. I can't go running around arresting people just on your say-so. First how do we know it was his cattle? Did you see them in your field? You got any eye-witnesses to testify that his stock ate your corn?"

Bendorf's rage flamed anew.

"Don't be a fool, Henry. What you trying to hedge for? Whose beef could it have been if there ain't any others in the country?"

"Another thing, this man—Frake I think his name is—hasn't got a head of stock anywhere near your land. He's located way over the other side. You mean to tell me he drove his cattle six or seven miles just to graze them on your corn?"

"I don't know what he did, but the corn is plumb ruined!"

Dalton laid a placating hand on Bendorf's shoulder. "Tell you what—you just ride on home and cool down a little and I'll mosy out and have a talk with this Frake. You don't want to have anybody arrested until you think it over a little."

Bendorf shook off the hand. He backed away, raising his fist. "So this is the kind of law we got in Ngania. A yellow-back marshal without guts enough to make an arrest..."

"Now Sam—"

"Well you don't have to bother. I'll do my own calling. You just sit here in your office and collect your pay."

Bendorf stormed out of the office. He was back on his *goff* and off down the street before Dalton appeared on the small porch of the building.

"Don't you go off half-cocked, Sam!" Dalton yelled. "You haven't got the right to maybe kill someone over what was probably an accident!"

Bendorf could hardly have heard the warning, but several gaping onlookers did. They gathered around, watching the departure of Bendorf, and Dalton said, "That man's gone plumb crazy. Acts like he's out for blood."

Halfway to where he was going, Bendorf was forced to slow down to a walk. His *goff* had begun to stagger and was showing signs of collapse. As he approached the place, two other riders were pounding along in his wake. When they had him in sight, they slowed down to move at a more leisurely pace.

Bendorf jumped from his *goff* and ran the last hundred yards. Just as he got there, the door opened and two men came out—Frake and Tip Snead.

"Which one of you is the boss? Which owns that herd of cattle?"

"What's the trouble, friend?" Frake rumbled. "I own some cattle. What about them?"

"They ruint my corn—that's what about 'em! Your damn herd tromped my whole crop into the ground, and it's going to cost you plenty!"

FRAKE RAISED his eyes and squinted across the prairie at the two approaching men. There was a calculating look on his face. He glanced at Snead—a glance full of silent meaning—and then walked slowly toward Bendorf.

"You're too excited, neighbor. If I was you I'd simmer down a little so we can talk this over."

Snead grinned in open contempt. "Yeah—I'd do that if I was you, neighbor. It isn't healthy to come around accusing people of ruining crops."

Snead moved off to the left, casually. His sneer had not been missed by Bendorf. It inflamed the man anew.

"It was deliberate! That's what it was!" Bendorf yelled. "What do you want to break me and starve my wife and kids for?"

He still spoke to Frake. Snead had circled and was standing behind him. Frake moved close to Bendorf. Frake was scowling now and the two approaching men on *goffs* were close enough to identify.

Frake pushed close to Bendorf. "You son-of-a—!"

Frake's arms were high up and his gun side turned toward Bendorf. A pyro-gun hung there invitingly.

In a frenzy, the maddened Bendorf snatched at the gun. Instantly, behind him, Snead shook his arm downward in a stiff motion. A knife slid along the inner side of his forearm and into the palm of his open-hand. His arm came up—flashed downward again—and a silver streak flew toward Bendorf's back.

Bendorf stiffened. The gun he'd snatched from Frake's holster was clutched for a moment in his hand. Then the gun dropped to the ground and Bendorf wilted down on top of it. Out on the prairie the two men whipped into a gallop, covered three swift furlongs and were in the yard.

Frake had not moved. He said, "Hello, Bates. We had a little trouble here. This pilgrim came prancing in on us yelling for blood. He tried to grab my gun and Snead nailed him. Saved my life, Snead did."

Bates stared down at the dead man. "I wonder what got into him?" he said. "By the way—meet Henry Dalton, marshal of Ngania."

The men exchanged nods and Bates went on, "Henry came and told me Bendorf had been to see him and that he was on the rampage. Something about his corn crop being ruined. We thought he was heading this way so we followed along. Looks as though we're too late."

"If Snead hadn't been on the alert, you'd have found me dead instead of Bendorf," Frake growled.

Bates had dismounted, but Dalton stayed on his *goff*, saying nothing. Expressionless, he watched Snead bend over and pull the knife from Bendorf's back. The knife had gone in almost to the hilt. Snead had to exert considerable pressure to get it loose.

"It's too bad," Bates said. "A damn shame that a man flies off the handle like that. He has a wife and two kids." Bates sighed. "Guess it's up to me to see that they get back home."

He turned to Dalton. "Henry, you'd better ride back to town and round up a jury to hear the evidence. Bring them back here and we'll hold an inquest. In the meantime don't touch the body."

"We'll keep it legal, huh?" Frake asked.

There was a hint of mockery in his voice; a touch of contempt so faint that it evidently escaped all but Bates.

Bates turned away and looked up at Dalton. "Get going," he ordered. "I'll wait here. Hurry it up, now."

Like an obedient child, Dalton kneed his *goff* around and started back toward Ngania. Bates watched until Dalton was well on his way. Then he turned to Snead. "Get a blanket and throw it over him," he said harshly. "I'm going to water my *goff*."

Snead went into the house. When he returned, Bates was already leading his animal across the corral toward the trough near the well at the far end.

Snead covered the corpse and straightened up. There was amusement in his voice as he said, "Looks like the big boss gets a little disturbed at the sight of blood."

FRANK BATES had only wanted to be alone for a few minutes in order to assemble his scattered thoughts.

This initial foray in his land grabbing scheme had not gone according to his plan. He had not anticipated a killing and he wanted to ascertain the effect of that killing upon his own mind.

He was rather surprised to find himself taking it so calmly. Bendorf was dead and his land would revert to the bank. Of these two facts, Bates found himself far more satisfied by the latter than he was disturbed by the former. Already his brain was planning ahead. He would send Mrs. Bendorf and her children back to Terra—shoulder all the expense himself—so that no one could point a finger at him. The bank would take over the land, quietly, and that would be that.

A life for two hundred acres.

Bates contemplated this development with inward calm. But in the mind of every man there is an independent intelligence that will not be blinded nor biased. That intelligence spoke to Frank Bates now. It said, "You've stepped over the line. Up to this point you were merely a sharp dealer. You were merely clever and you used your legal advantages to further your ambitions. But you're over the line now. You've thrown other men's lives into the pot. You've stepped across the divide, Bates. How does it feel?"

It didn't feel bad at all. In fact a new surge of power came to Frank Bates as the moral restraints slipped away. After all, why should he be held back by those with less astuteness, less ambition than he?

His conscience was now stilled forever except for one final, tiny twinge. That came three weeks later when he said goodbye to Mrs. Bendorf. The widow was seated in Bates' own carriage in front of Bates' own bank, and her two children were with her. Bates had arranged that she be driven cross-country to the nearest freighter head. As she looked at him, there were tears in her eyes and her hand clutched his warmly.

"Thank you for all you've done," she said, and her voice was choked. "Thank you very much."

Bates' last twinge of conscience came and went.

He returned to his office and found satisfaction in a sudden feeling of contempt. These squatters! Men so stupid and spineless had no right to own land. The sooner they were cleaned out, the better. This vast planet was the heritage of the strong...

CHAPTER NINE

TIP SNEAD was comfortably and happily drunk. His winnings at the poker table of the Golden King amounted to some fifty credits and that made it a nice evening all around.

Toward midnight he pocketed his money, had one more drink, and left the saloon. He got his *goff* from the stable, waved a cheery goodbye, and set out for home.

His pinto had learned the way by this time and there was little need of direction. Snead let his reins hang loose and slumped forward in the saddle. His body moved to the rhythm of the animal's jog and he drifted into a doze.

The voice awakened him. It was a sharp voice he had never before heard. "Snead—rein up!"

He pulled the pinto to a halt and looked about into the darkness, the sleep still in his eyes. On each side a *goff* crowded close and before he was quite awake, his reins were snatched away and his holster was emptied.

"Wha—what is this? A holdup?"

The only answer was a short laugh coming out of the darkness, and cold fear flushed through Tip Snead. He said, "I won a little in the game. You can have it. It's in my right-hand pocket."

"He wears a knife in his sleeve. Get it!" A different voice clipped out these words and Snead was jostled again. Two hands grasped his right arm and tore open the button holding his sleeve. The knife snapped from its spring holder.

"Got it."

"All right. Tie his hands."

"Do you have to tie a man up to rob him?" Snead whined.

"Your money stays in your pocket. Don't worry about it. We aren't thieves."

Snead turned cold. Sickness welled into his stomach.

There were five of them. Five shapes in the dimness that rode close around Snead as his *goff* was hauled off the road and led across the prairie at a tangent. There was no uncertainty here. These men evidently knew why they had come and where they were going.

"What's this about?" Snead yelled. "Where we headed?"

There was no answer.

"For God's sake! Talk…somebody! Say something!"

He could have been pleading with deaf-mutes.

"Answer me, damn it! What is this?"

No reply, and Snead went swiftly to pieces.

"Look! It wasn't my fault. I only did what any other man would do. He tried to snatch Frake's gun and I had to get him or he'd have gotten Frake. A man has to be loyal to his friends! You'd have done the same thing. Any of you."

The clop-clop-clop of the hoof-beats increased in tempo as the cavalcade went into a trot. The silent men traveled north and slightly west with their prisoner. Eventually Cotter's Creek blocked their path. They sheered eastward, following its course until they came to a grove.

"It was all legal," Snead screamed. "I tell you it was legal. There was an inquest and a jury and they said I done right."

For the first time, one of the men answered him. "We know all about that. We know who was on the jury and who told them to bring the verdict they brought. Hangers-on in the Ngania drinking halls. We knew Sam too, and he wasn't the kind of a man to kill unless he was driven to it."

"But you can't—aw please, men! Give a feller a chance! I'll get out of the country! I'll ride and keep right on going. You can't hang a man in cold blood!"

THE ROPE came from somewhere to settle around his neck from behind. He screamed a thin scream and tried to throw himself out of the saddle but there were *goffs* on each side, hemming him in.

Perspiration made his sick white face shine in the faint starlight.

"Give a poor devil a chance!"

The rope was over a limb above his head.

"It was Frake. He's the boss—Frake is, I tell you. He made me do it. Frake'd killed me if I hadn't. What could I do?"

There was slack in the rope—enough for a two-foot drop. The riders on either side of him faded back. A moment of silence and the sharp sound of a hand slapping the rump of Snead's *goff*.

"Ghaaaaaa. Aggghhhhh."

Snead sought to hold the stirrups but they slipped from his insteps. The *goff* danced ahead some twenty feet where it stopped and turned. It snorted and there were no other sounds in the grove.

After a time Snead stopped kicking. Then the five men rode away—in different directions over the prairie.

Snead's body dangled from the willow limb, turning slowly in the darkness.

MEL DORKEN came awake with a start. He opened his eyes and wondered what had broken his slumber. Through the wall he could hear the even heavy breathing of Frake in the next room.

Dorken lay still for a moment. Then it came again—the impatient snorting of a *goff*. The man swung his feet to the floor and reached for his pants. He drew on his boots, pulled his gun from its holster, and went out through the back door into the yard.

The snort was repeated, along with the sound of a hoof scraping the ground, and Dorken saw a large shadow by the corral gate. He approached in long strides.

A *goff*. Snead's, with no rider and its reins wrapped around the saddle horn.

Dorken scowled. What the devil had happened to Tip? Dead drunk and off his *goff* somewhere back down the road? That was probably it. Frake ought to lay the law down to the little saddle tramp. He had a weakness for liquor and he was dangerous. He'd kill somebody one of these days under the wrong circumstances and there'd be hell in camp.

Dorken unsaddled the beast and turned it into the corral. The *goff* galloped off toward the feed rack, and Dorken trailed back toward the house. No use waking up Frake, he thought. Tip would come straggling along, maybe before dawn if he slept off his night on the town.

The big outlaw looked up at the stars and forgot about Snead. He was thinking of a girl—a slim girl with blue eyes and yellow hair.

On the afternoon of the following day, Mel Dorken lounged by the hitching rack in front of the Golden King. He was watching a sorrel *goff* at another hitching rack down the street. Pretty soon a girl with golden hair would come out of the bank and fork that animal. Then—Dorken hoped—the girl would ride north as she had usually done before.

Her route had been—for the most part—along the eastern boundary of a section that had been homesteaded by an early hopeful and now in the possession of the Ngania Bank.

Then, at the creek, she would veer due east. Dorken had never been able to trace the girl to her destination, but that was not necessary for the purpose he had in mind. About three miles down the creek, she passed close to an abandoned shack in an otherwise deserted stretch of hilly country.

This was as far as Dorken's thinking carried him.

The man waited almost an hour and was about to give up, when Kay Bates appeared. She mounted and Dorken turned his back and was studying the doors of the Golden King when she rode by.

Several minutes later he grunted in satisfaction, climbed on his own *goff*, and left town, following a line northward and slightly to the east. Clear of Ngania, he put spurs to his *goff* and pounded over the land, straight toward a thronga grove he had in mind. This grove, not two hundred yards from the abandoned shack, would keep him covered until the girl got close enough.

There was no finesse involved in Dorken's plan. His approach would be as elemental as his desires and his purpose. Catching the girl unaware, he could ride down the sorrel before she would be able to react. Surprise was in his favor.

He reached the grove and edged his *goff* into a thick patch of thronga that formed a wall cutting off the heavier section of the grove. He dismounted and took up a post at the outer edge of the thicket.

THE GIRL was not yet in sight, but she would come from the west along the creek bank, to pass within two hundred feet of Dorken.

The outlaw growled under his breath. This was the hard part—the waiting, here in the grove, with his trap set. Her arrival would be a signal for the snapping of a spring inside Dorken's mind—the unleashing of a tiger. It would probably all be over, he thought, before the girl knew what had happened. In no time at all.

Strangely, the project was not as suicidal for Dorken as it appeared. This yellow-haired dream was no scullery maid. She came of fine family, the daughter of Ngania's leading citizen. There was a certain restraint in such people that could easily work to Dorken's benefit. It was an even chance that no one would ever hear of this incident on the prairie. Dorken sensed that a girl of Kay Bates' background would think twice before she accused him, because the accusation would do untold damage to her own reputation.

If it worked out this way, Dorken's position would be unchanged. He could go on as before. If the girl pointed a finger in public... Dorken shrugged. He'd ridden out of such spots before. He could do it again.

She was coming now—a mile up the creek. Dorken could see a small speck moving closer. The speck became a *goff* and a rider. Then the *goff* became a high-stepping sorrel and the rider was clearly a girl.

Of the girl, Dorken saw first what had originally set his emotions astir—shining yellow hair. Odd, he thought, that a simple thing like that could set a man's instincts afire. He went back into the thronga patch and mounted his *goff* and brought it just to the outer edge of the grove.

Now he waited.

The *goff* came dancing along, urged by an impatience in the girl. Her eyes were trained dead ahead as though they had no time for anything except what lay at the end of the journey.

Two hundred yards—a hundred. Dorken crouched in his saddle ready to spur into the open.

Then the girl jerked her mount to a sudden halt. She was staring at the thronga grove as though she had caught sight of the devil himself crouching there.

Dorken was thrown off balance by this development. She'd seen him! What the hell! Did the girl have eyes that bored right through wood? She'd done the impossible. She'd caught sight of him...

A scream ripped the air and Kay Bates was down over the neck of the sorrel and the *goff* was flying by the grove at a speed that would have left Dorken's mount practically standing still.

In a flash she was gone, but not until another scream followed the first, to thin out as the sorrel sped over the red prairie.

Dorken cursed. As a vent for his rage, he pulled tight on his reins, arching his mount's neck, and began beating the animal on the head with his doubled fist. It was the *goff!* That was all it could have been. The *goff* had made some sound that the girl had caught. The fact that Dorken hadn't caught the sound—seated even as he was on the *goff* itself—did not enter into his reasoning.

The beast reared and plunged and finally Dorken gave off beating it and rode straight off across the prairie toward Ngania.

After he had calmed down somewhat, a certain strangeness in the incident came to his mind. That yellow-haired skirt was certainly touchy. After all, what had she seen? A man and a *goff* in the thronga grove. It was enough to startle her no doubt, but it appeared that her fright was a little over done. Was she in the habit of screaming bloody murder every time a bug jumped across her path?

Dorken mulled the thing over as he rode back to Ngania. After a while he felt better. There would be another time.

KAY BATES buried her white face in Cory Balleau's shoulder. Her body, trembling in his arms, pressed close to him. Her voice was muffled by his clothing.

"A body hanging there from a tree. Its eyes were bulging and the tongue—oh lord!"

Cory put a finger under the girl's chin and raised her head. "But you don't know who it was?"

"No. I didn't wait. I came away from there."

"And the man on the *goff*. You said you saw a man hiding in the thronga."

"Not hiding. I looked back and saw him come out on this side of the creek. The body was on the other side in the grove—beyond the thronga thicket. I saw it from up the creek. And Cory—do you know who the man was—the one on the *goff*?"

"Who?"

"The same one I met out on the prairie that day—the one that scared me so."

"The cattleman."

"That's right. I've seen him in town since then. He's with that Mr. Frake who owns the cattle that tramped down Sam Bendorf's corn."

"Not the knife-thrower who killed Bendorf?"

"No, but one of that gang."

Cory pushed Kay away from him and scanned her face; "You're over your fright a little now. You'd better head for home. I'll have to get Uncle John and ride up to that grove. We can't just leave a man hanging there."

"I suppose not. Be careful, though, Cory. Be awfully careful."

When the sorrel was a spot off on the prairie, the youth moved slowly toward his own *goff*. His mind shrank away from the situation. The knowledge of a hanged man up the creek had a peculiar effect upon him and he was trying to analyze that effect.

In itself, the corpse at the end of a rope didn't mean too much. Beyond natural curiosity it stirred him not at all. But there was something else, a feeling that the incident engendered.

It was as if his subconscious mind was aware of not only all that had happened, but of what was going to happen and was trying to get through to him with a warning; as though his destiny was already foreordained and the hanging of this man—whoever he turned out to be—was another cog in an ever-moving chain, driving him onward toward something from which he shrank.

It seemed a part of a planned whole. There had been other cogs in this chain and he remembered them. And in each cog, fate used the same pawn; in each incident loomed the sinister figure of Mel Dorken.

Dorken seated astride a victim, gouging out his eyes; Dorken walking into the Golden King and sending a cold shock through Cory Balleau; Dorken astride a *goff* on the prairie to frighten Kay Bates; Dorken emerging from a thronga grove in which hung the body of a man. Always the same man. Always this Mel Dorken.

There was a mysticism in the mind of Cory Balleau that responded to the seeming diabolical intent of this pattern.

At this moment, Cory Balleau was afraid of Mel Dorken. He was afraid of the symbol that the man had become. A symbol of evil destiny.

CHAPTER TEN

"THERE WERE at least four of them—maybe half a dozen," Frake said. "They caught him on his way out of town. They brought him here because it's the nearest tree—and they strung him up."

Frake's face was tight with unconcealed rage. Astride a *goff* beside Frake, Mel Dorken sullenly eyed the lynching tree. A two-foot length of rope was still hanging from the limb.

Frank Bates chewed nervously on a cold cigar and Henry Dalton, the other member of the group, seemed bewildered, a man out of his depth.

"You still haven't told us what you were doing here, Dorken," Bates said.

The big outlaw scowled darkly. "I told you I wasn't here. I wasn't no place near this grove and I never have been 'til now."

"My daughter doesn't lie..."

"She could make a mistake, though. She was probably so damn scared she didn't know who she saw. And if we're going into that—what was she doing here?"

"That's beside the point and none of your affair. This country is free and my daughter can ride anywhere she wants to."

"All this palaver is doing us no good," Frake said. "It doesn't matter whether Dorken was here or not. We know five or six men strung Tip up and we know what we've got to do."

"There isn't much we can do, is there?" Dalton asked. "With no witnesses I'd say we're kind of helpless unless someone talks."

Frake threw him a look of rank contempt. Then, wheeling his *goff*, Frake made a quick beckoning motion with his head, and started away from the grove at a quick trot.

Bates, at whom the command was pointed, drew away from the other two and moved close to Frake. At a distance beyond earshot, Dorken and Dalton followed.

"Looks like you misjudged things a little," Frake said.

Bates flushed, resenting the superior tone. "Misjudged what?"

"Let's not dance around. You figured these nesters would sit back and let you pick them off one by one. You didn't rate them for any guts at all. Now your cute little plan's back-fired."

Bates admitted—but only to himself—that he was shaken by this grim turn of events; shaken to the core. In all his calculations as to possible results of the operation, he had anticipated nothing like this.

NOW HE REALIZED a truth he had not been aware of. These men—these nesters—respected the law and bowed to legal dictates. If they borrowed money on their land and ran into hard luck, they paid off without a murmur and sought their fortunes elsewhere. But they dealt in the coin of the realm and if that coin was murder they paid off in kind.

"Night riders," Bates said. "What are things coming to in Ngania? Have we gone beyond law and order?"

Frake spat in disgust. "If there's anything I hate it's a hypocrite! My name's Frake—remember? I'm in with you on this deal. Let's talk sense or to hell with it."

Bates didn't answer for some time. Then he asked, "What are your ideas?"

"That depends on you. Your hand's been called, man, and you do one of two things. If you're yellow you pull in your horns and let this thing die down. In that case you and I do a little settling up and I go on my way." Frake leaned outward from his saddle and looked straight into Bates' eyes. "And when I leave this town," He added grimly, "I take something with me."

Bates thought that over for a moment. "And the alternative?"

"The alternative is war."

"And which do you suggest?"

"The last. You're in a perfect position to win. It won't be a picnic and maybe there'll be soldiers in the picture before it's over, but you're in shape to keep the law on your side right from the start. Every move you've made so far has been legal, even the Bendorf killing. It's the squatters that are outside the law."

"You feel that we hold all the cards, then?"

"Of course we do. First thing, you get rid of that weak-knee you've got for a marshal and I take his job. Then somebody gets hung for this lynching. We build a scaffold right in Ngania and string them up at high noon. That's the way you keep law and order."

The fear in Bates' heart began to subside. What had he been worrying about? A lynch-mob prowling the night wasn't an indication of strength. Lynching was an act of weakness—of desperation. Such resistance would break in the face of determined reprisal. Frake was right.

But another point caught and held in Bates' mind. He'd have to come out in the open now. He would be hated and feared by his fellow citizens. He would walk the streets of Ngania a marked man. No more pussyfooting. This was war.

"I think we'll go forward boldly," Bates said.

Frake smiled. When he did that his lips came up off stained teeth and gave him a savage look. "How soon can you get rid of Dalton?"

"Give me a week. Then I'll see that he's displaced for lack of action in running down the lynchers. I think I can persuade him to go back where he came from."

"Good."

"And there's another thing."

Frake waited.

"Those two homesteaders who brought Snead's body in—the Balleaus. I loaned the elder Balleau some money. There was a three-Marsmonth clause in the contract and the money is due now. He can't pay of course."

Frake's eyes scanned the face of the other. "You mean the man borrowed money like that? Nobody'd do that without knowing where the cash was coming from to pay with."

"It wasn't exactly like that. Balleau was under the impression he was borrowing for a longer period."

Frake grinned again. "I see. Another chunk of land for Frank Bates."

Bates ignored that. "No doubt there'll be trouble even though I've got a competent witness to swear Balleau knew what he was doing. My teller witnessed the signature. The contract is perfectly legal."

There was a touch of admiration in Frake's glance. "How'd you manage that?"

"That's not important. The thing is, Balleau will probably be stubborn. He may have to be evicted by force. That's a job you'll inherit with your new office."

Frake pondered for a moment. "That fits in pretty good. We might as well let them all know that the honeymoon's over in these parts. Any excuse to get rough is fine."

"Give me a week," Bates said once again.

THE BODY of Tip Snead, at Frake's direction, was placed, in the window of Carter's Farm Emporium. Also at his direction, a printed card was placed beside the open coffin:

THIS MAN WAS HUNG BY COWARDS!

The due processes of law have been flouted in the town of Ngania by skulking nightriders who took this man and hung him to a tree and watched him strangle to death. Are we going to allow this kind of thing in Ngania? The next victim may be you or one of your loved ones. Once started, rats of this kind are only stopped by a pellet. We Terran citizens, demand that our marshal apprehend these killers without delay. We demand action!

"That'll clear the way so you can get rid of Dalton without any trouble," Frake told Bates. "It won't be your fault when the citizens start grousing."

With the display of the body, a pall settled over the town. Men seemed to walk softer and the talk in the stores and the drinking halls was muted. Fear was there in the streets and every man and woman felt the fear.

The body stayed there two days, after which time the proprietor of Carter's demanded its removal, saying that his business was at a standstill. The women of Ngania avoided the store. They even gave the window a wide berth, circling out into the street as they passed.

Cory Balleau was probably more sensitive of the fear than anyone else. Yet not fear exactly; in his heart he felt great dread of the future. There was a certain bewilderment in his mind. He could not displace the feeling that this was only the beginning of something that would affect him deeply. Within him was a sense that the tides of time were sweeping him forward and that he was helpless to resist, driving him relentlessly toward a destiny not of his own making.

John Balleau held himself aloof from the trouble that had descended upon Ngania. After carrying the body of Tip Snead to town, he returned to his beloved land, giving no time to the gossip, the excitement, and the upheaval in the town.

He had seed and tools and, in the processes of his thinking, enough to make any man content. He worked tirelessly.

As he tilled the acres, he spent a great deal of time thinking about Cory. The youth was changing. He had grown quieter and yet there was a renewed restlessness that John Balleau could discern underneath. John Balleau's attempts to urge Cory into a social life went pretty much to naught. During his leisure hours, Cory enjoyed roaming the prairies, following the creek and journeying to the rocky hill country further west.

But always alone—and that was the thing that worried the elder Balleau. The laughter and happiness that should be a part of youth were not to be found in long solitary treks.

He'd have to talk to Cory about it—dig deeper—find out what was troubling the lad—

KAY BATES slid off the sorrel mare and was eased to the ground by Cory's hands under her armpits. She moved close to him, rubbed the tip of her nose against his, and laughed.

"Cold nose," she said, "cold heart."

Cory turned away, evidently not noticing the kiss that was offered. He took three steps and dropped to the sod bordering the creek. He lay belly down with his head over the bank's edge, his face reflected in the still backwater.

A moment later he saw the questioning face of Kay Bates in the water beside his own.

"Why so quiet?" she asked.

"I've been thinking. I've been doing a lot of thinking. There's trouble in Ngania—bad trouble. I don't like it."

"But it won't affect us," the girl said quickly.

"How do we know it won't? Who knows what direction trouble will take?"

She studied his reflection, her own face sober. "You seem so worried lately. Is it something you know? Something you haven't told me?"

"No it's nothing—just—" He turned and looked deep into her blue eyes. "Well—I'm not the one for you. You've got to stop coming out here. We've got to quit seeing each other like this or the trouble *will* come our way—trouble for you."

She sat very still without answering. Then she spun her lithe body, pulled him around with her and he was prone on his back and her breast hard against his. She was looking straight into his eyes. She said, "Cory—are you in love with me?"

He returned the look but with a vagueness in his eyes. "I don't know. Maybe. I guess I don't know what love is. Are you in love with me?"

"Always and forever."

"What is it then? How do you feel? Tell me."

Again she was silent as though seeking words with which to give her answer. Finally she said, "I guess every girl is different and maybe, with every girl, the feeling isn't the same. With me love is—well, just everything. I know there will only be one person I'll ever love. I don't know how I know that, but I do. And I don't know what it is. I only feel it and I think of it in two ways—having it, and protecting it."

She stopped to kiss him—a casual, unpassionate kiss—and then went on:

"With me there can be no room for love and reservations at the same time. I belong to the person I love and that person is you. I belong to you anywhere, in any way, at anytime. There isn't anything you could ask of me that you couldn't have now or tomorrow or twenty years from now if it's within my power to give."

Her body was against his and the wonder came sharply into his mind: Why can't I put my arms around her? What's blocking me off from what any man on two legs would give ten years of his life to have?

"Please don't misunderstand, darling," she said. "I'm sure that I'm not a 'slut.' I'm not immoral, because it's only *you*. Can you understand that? You...you...you... I want marriage, but I'm not afraid of love. I don't have to be protected by a piece of paper."

"Will you marry me, Kay?" Cory asked.

And he thought, *I wish I could really mean that. I wish that I could really want to marry her.*

She smiled down at him. "Silly! If that were possible don't you think I'd have wriggled that question out of you long ago? I'd have been able to make you ask that a week after I found that I wanted you."

"Why isn't it possible?"

SHE STRAIGHTENED now, drew her body away from his, and sat cross-legged beside him. She stared out over the prairie.

"Because of my father."

"Doesn't he want you to get married?"

Her reply was indirect. "You see, I know my father. I know him even better than he knows himself. I've watched him take the land away from the settlers and I've seen the cruelty underneath his scheming. He wants me to marry some Terran man. To him I've just another asset to be used to the best advantage. He's very jealous of his assets."

"Tell him you don't want to do that. Tell him you want to marry me."

"He'd kill you."

"He'd *what?* What did you say?"

"I said he'd kill you. Oh he wouldn't do it himself of course, but he'd find a way. He's surrounding himself with some terrible, ruthless men. My father is too clever to commit his own murders. But he has a scheming mind that would manipulate things until you were dead. I know that as surely as I'm alive."

Cory was struck speechless by the flat, cold denunciation. He stared at the girl. She said, "You think that's horrible, don't you?" She returned his look and her words came in dull monotone. "Maybe it is, but I know I'm right and if anything happened to you I'd die—inside of me my heart would shrivel up into a husk and I wouldn't be alive any more."

"I think you must be wrong," he said, gently.

"I'm not wrong. But maybe things will change. I keep praying that they will. But meanwhile, no other girl will get you—I'll scratch the eyes out of any who ever try." There was no smile on her face. "I mean that," she said.

Eight days after the discovery of Tip Snead's body, Henry Dalton handed in his badge and the office of Marshal of Ngania was vacant for fifteen minutes.

After Frake was sworn in, Frank Bates made a short speech to the assembled citizens: "…and we can rest assured that law and order have an able champion in the person of our new marshal. I am confident that he will be successful in his campaign to bring the killers in our midst to justice. We wish him every success and offer every cooperation."

Frake's opening statement was short and to the point: "As Marshal of Ngania, I personally guarantee complete immunity to the first of the lynch mob who walks into my office and makes a confession. Also, Mr. Bates has offered a thousand dollars reward for information leading to the capture of the night riders."

Frank Bates was somewhat surprised at this last. It was the first he'd heard of any reward. Thinking it over, though, he decided that it was an excellent idea.

CHAPTER ELEVEN

THERE WERE five men in the group that dismounted at the gate of John Balleau's place, and skirted the neat house to come into view from the corral. They were Frank Bates, Marshal Frake, Deputy Marshal Mel Dorken, and two spare deputies of less imposing proportions.

John Balleau had just turned his team into the back pasture and was coming forward across the corral. Upon seeing the men, he stopped short and stared for a moment, a slight frown on his face. What did this mean? There was no reason for a bevy of armed men to be waiting for him in his own back yard.

He continued on toward the pond and crossed the bridge at the narrow point. He approached the group silently, his unasked question reflecting in his face.

"How are you, Balleau?" Bates asked by way of greeting.

"No complaint. What can I do for you gentlemen?"

Bates took the cold cigar from his mouth. He appeared to be a trifle surprised. "You seem to have a short memory, Balleau. I've been expecting you to show up in town, but when you stayed away it made me rather uneasy—a banker's mind, you know—so I thought I'd drop out and pick up the principal on your note."

Balleau registered sheer unbelief. "You *what?*"

"I think I spoke clearly. Your note is two weeks overdue. It's hardly businesslike to let it run. I came out to clean it up."

A wave of quick weakness swept over Balleau. For a moment there was a blur before his eyes. This was some sort of a bad dream! But his eyes cleared and the men were still there and Bates was saying, "What's come over you, man? You act as though you don't remember borrowing money from me. Don't you feel well?"

Balleau choked for words. His gaze moved helplessly to where Dorken had stepped casually away from the group. Dorken stood to one side. His legs were spread wide and his arms folded as he watched the farce through narrowed, lazy eyes.

"But—but the only money I borrowed from you was on an eighteen Marsmonth basis. The term has hardly begun! I don't understand."

Bates' words came as cold as dripping, ice pellets. "I don't know what kind of a game you're trying to play, but that will hardly wash. If you can read English you can check your copy of the document that you signed before a reliable witness. It clearly reads that the time limit was three months. As I remember it you wanted the money for machinery—a short-term loan—I took it for granted that you had a method of repaying."

There was an odd glaze over Balleau's eyes. Like a man in a dream—stiff-legged—he walked toward the back door. He opened it and went inside.

The document in question was in his bedroom, in a box with other documents. He'd taken it from his pocket that day, upon returning home, and hadn't even read it. Now, as panic edged into his mind, he realized that he should have read it. But there on the table in Bates' office at the bank, he'd checked the important points. He'd seen the words eighteen months from date very plainly.

But like the tolling of a doom-bell was the knowledge within his mind that those words would not be on the document he now possessed.

He took the box from his dresser drawer. The paper was upon the very top of the pile inside. He unfolded it carefully as though it were fine glass that would break at a touch. There they were, four words: "three Marsmonths from date."

THE WORLD of John Balleau went spinning out from under him and he was whirling over and over in space. The period of faintness passed. The man's mind cleared again.

Thievery! Sheer bald-faced thievery! The gypsy switch in a place where a man took integrity for granted. Cold-blooded, legal robbery.

Something in John Balleau's mind snapped.

He flung open the closet door and reached inside. His hand came out holding a para-rifle. He threw down the lever. There were live pellets in the magazine. He slapped the lever back in place, his brain awhirl.

They wouldn't get away with it! There flashed before him a picture of the old place back on Terra—the desolation he'd seen from the hilltop when he'd returned to his last hope. He recalled the long trek skyward—a grave back on the Marsriver. The weary months and years.

They wouldn't get away with it. And he was standing in the doorway with the rifle flung up, covering the group.

"You thieving blackguards! Get off my property! Get off before I blow you all to hell where you belong! You'll, take this land over my dead body and if I die you'll all go with me! Get out!"

Mel Dorken, standing away to the left, was outside the lethal arc of the gun. His hand slipped down to his hip and came up holding a pyro gun. Balleau's eye caught the motion and the rifle swung around.

Dorken fired from the hip as Balleau pressed the switch of the para-rifle and leaped backward into the shelter of the kitchen.

The pellet hit and melted a rock at Dorken's feet and whined off across the corral.

Bates and the lawmen went into a quick and undignified retreat. They found shelter by using an angle of the house to cover their exodus and gathered in the partial shelter of a grove by the road.

Immediately a corner of a front window-plastic was pushed out and the barrel of the para-rifle appeared. "Over my dead body you'll take this land!" Balleau yelled, "Thieves! Thieves! Thieves!"

"Did you hit him, Mel?" Frake asked, scowling.

"I don't think so," the latter growled. "He moved too quick."

"I don't like this," Bates cut in. "I don't like it at all. We can't shoot the man down in cold blood."

Frake eyed the banker coldly. "Why not? He's resisting officers of the law. He endangered our lives with a deadly weapon. Why can't we shoot him?"

"It's too—too abrupt somehow. I just don't like it."

"You mean that Tip Snead's lynchers are still not captured and hung. You're thinking they might catch you some dark night and string you to a tree. That's it, isn't it?"

Bates reddened. "Nothing of the kind. But we didn't come out here to kill this man—"

"We came to steal his property."

"Quit putting words in my mouth. We're going back to town and give him a chance to cool off. When we come back we'll bring some impartial witnesses."

Frake shrugged. They remounted under the watchful eye of the rifle and hit the road for Ngania.

CORY BALLEAU loped in from the east, trying to beat the sun. He felt guilty at being away so long. There were chores to be done and he was hardly carrying his share of the load. His uncle worked all day and should find a meal waiting when he returned to the house.

Cory raced to the corral gate, stripped his *goff,* and slammed the gate behind it. He crossed the bridge at a run and pelted into the kitchen.

He stopped—sharply alert. Something was wrong. The house was deathly quiet and a path of dark red stained the floor. It led toward the front of the house. Cory followed it on tiptoe...

The trail ended in a pool and the body of John Balleau lay in the center of the pool. The blood had coursed down from a wound in his neck where a blood vessel had been charred.

John Balleau lay face downward, the fingers of one hand touching the butt of the para-rifle propped against the windowsill. The corner of the plastic had been broken out and the barrel of the rifle protruded.

Cory knelt in the blood and lifted his uncle, turned the limp body and cradled it in his arms. He held it there and looked down into the still face.

No need for close investigation. There was too much blood on the floor. John Balleau's body was empty of blood and therefore empty of life.

After a while, Cory got up from the floor, took the para-rifle and went to the corral. He saddled his *goff* and rode off down the road toward town. He gripped the rifle so tightly that his fingers ached. And his jaw muscles, hard and corded, ached also.

CORY BALLEAU rode up the main street of Ngania and dismounted in front of the marshal's office. He entered and found Frake sitting with his chair tilted back and one booted foot on his desk. Frake lowered the foot, glanced at the para-rifle under Cory's arm and then looked up at the youth's face.

"Somebody killed my uncle," Cory said.

At that instant the door opened and Frank Bates strode in. Bates asked, "What was that?"

Cory turned. "I said somebody killed my uncle."

Bates' shoulder jerked sharply as though from a sudden nervous disorder. He cursed inwardly. These accidents! These unforeseen occurrences that were forever darkening his plans! He turned his eyes to Frake. "Then Dorken's shot must have—" He stopped with some uncertainty.

Frake scowled and said to Cory, "We didn't know that, son. We went out to your uncle's place to collect a claim against him—a legal claim. He resisted with a gun; that very gun you're carrying. There was a shot fired but your uncle ran back into the house and we thought he was all right. Maybe after we left—"

"It was Dorken then?" Cory's voice held no emotion. It was a casual question made up of dully spoken words.

"Well...Dorken fired a shot—to defend himself—but we—"

Cory turned and went out of the office into the street. He had little doubt as to where he'd find Mel Dorken. He walked west toward the Golden King. He pushed in through the batwings and looked up and down the bar.

Dorken was there, standing alone at the far end. There was a bottle and a glass in front of him. Cory walked up to him and Dorken turned. Cory poked the barrel of the para-rifle into his belly.

"I hear you killed my uncle," Cory said.

Genuine surprise on Dorken's hairy face. "That's a lie!"

"Did you fire a shot at him this afternoon?"

"I fired but—"

"I'm going to kill you."

Dorken's eyes flicked downward. The tenseness in his body faded as it had come. This thickheaded plow son! Holding a gun right close on a man with the switch locked. What could you expect of a squatter's kid?

Dorken pushed the gun aside and slammed his fist into Cory's face. Cory's body bent like a reed in the wind. His hands flew up and the gun fell to the floor. Cory reeled backward, struggling for balance.

He went down and Dorken was waiting for him at the spot where he hit the floor. Dorken's foot came back and swung out in a vicious arc squarely into Cory's, side. The boy screamed, rolled over and came to his knees, head hanging.

Dorken reached down and lifted him by his shirt. Dorken swung him around and slammed the fist again. Cory skidded across the floor to stop against the wall.

The rage of Dorken seemed to increase rather than diminish. He hurled a kick against the boy's spine, bringing a groan.

THEN THERE were men around Dorken—the barkeep and the poker dealer and a couple of hangers-on.

"That's enough, Dorken! For God's sake! You don't want to kill him! He's only a kid!"

They were holding his arms and it was as though they wrestled with an enraged grizzly. He shook them off and moved toward Cory and they threw themselves between.

"Get Frake," the barkeep yelled. "Somebody get the marshal!"

Dorken shook them off and picked Cory up and smashed a blow at his nose. But Dorken swung too low and the fist crashed against Cory's throat. The youth dropped, gagging for breath.

"Dorken! That's enough! You kill the kid and it's murder!"

"I'll blind him!"

Dorken lunged as the batwings swung and Frake walked into the Saloon.

"What's going on?"

"Stop him," the barkeep yelled. "We don't want a killing in here!"

Dorken was on his knees over Cory.

Frake took three long steps, hooked his arm around Dorken's neck and jerked him backward. Dorken rolled prone, his eyes ever seeking Cory.

"Get him out of here," Frake said. "Get the kid out. I'll handle Dorken."

The barkeep and the poker dealer dragged Cory and lifted him. They moved him toward the door and Frake crashed into the now-erect Dorken. His low words were flung against the wild man's ear, "You son of a bitch! You want to wreck everything? You want to get *us* lynched? Quiet down or I'll blast the top of your head off!"

The temperature of Dorken's brain cooled swiftly. He pulled away from Frake and dragged a hand across his own mouth. He said, "The stinkin' little tramp! Let's get a drink."

FRANK BATES arrived at his home rather late that evening. He recounted the events of the day at dinner;

recounted them sadly, as though such things disturbed him. "...I think Dorken would have killed the lad if Frake hadn't gotten there in time. Good man, Frake."

Kay Bates was on her feet. "Where did Cory go?"

Her father got up slowly. "Why, home I suppose. Where else would he go?"

Kay ran to the stairs and up to the second floor. Her father left the dining room, genuinely mystified. He waited at the foot of the staircase.

As Kay came pelting down, Frank Bates asked, "What in heaven's name got into you? Where are you going?"

"I'm going to find him. Leave me alone!"

"But you don't even know him."

Kay's smile was a thing of light and triumph. "Oh, don't I? You'd be surprised who I know and what I know. Get out of my way!"

Bates flared. "Silence! You're speaking to your father, young lady. I don't know what this is all about, but I damn soon *will* know. Come into my study..."

She quieted then, appeared to become more quiet inside, but she made no move to obey.

"Dad—Dad! Why can't we—oh—"

"Come into my study."

She hardened again. "Get out of my way!"

Frank Bates put his arms around her, snatched her roughly. Then he got the surprise of his life.

He could as well have laid his hands on a she-cougar defending her young. Kay screamed, flung her body and pumped her arms in violent motions. Bates sprang back, his hands over his face. When he lowered them, his daughter was gone.

He stood there with the blood running down his face from the deep furrows clawed there by slashing fingernails. Flesh hung at the bottoms of these furrows.

Bates stared at the blood on his hands.

Kay Bates rode the dark prairie in a straight line. The *goff's* hooves pounded the night. Filled with energy, the animal hugged the ground and ate the distance with long, joyous strides. The pace created a wind that cooled Kay Bates' lovely face and dealt roughly with her hair, brushing it loose and flinging it out behind her.

When the *goff* sought to lessen her speed, Kay applied a quirt and the *goff* leaped forward with a surprised snort. There was no letup until Kay flung herself from the saddle in front of the dark Balleau house.

Dead quiet. No life. Only a brooding silence...the silence of defeat. The house itself seemed to have taken on the hopeless mood of the vanquished.

Kay entered the dark kitchen. She struck a match and found a quartz lamp to light. On the floor was the dark streak. Dried blood. She followed it through the house, carrying the lamp above her head. The streak ended in the black dry pool by the broken window.

The girl carried the lamp out into the still night along the path that skirted the house.

"Cory! Cory!"

She crossed the footbridge and was in the corral. No sounds.

"Cory!"

Kay forgot the lamp and as her foot struck a clod, the lamp teetered and fell to the ground. Kay ran to the corral gate. It stood open.

Then from off in the darkness came the rattle of a *goff*. Kay's sorrel answered, and Kay called again, "Cory! Cory! Darling—it's me! Kay!"

The invisible *goff* snorted and Kay knew. The animal was wandering the prairie. The Balleau stock had been turned loose to shift for itself.

That meant—

But the girl refused to believe. He was there— somewhere out there hurt and bleeding. The thought drove her to panic.

"Cory! Cory!"

Up the creek maybe, at their old place. That's where he would go. Her heart swelled in gratitude for the thought. She raced to the sorrel and pounded westward along the creek. The miles rolled under the sorrel and Kay was there by the bend where the waters widened.

He's here somewhere—lying here hurt, waiting for me.

"Cory!"

The throngas murmured in sympathy, a vagrant breeze bringing their message. Kay flung herself to the sod. She knew now. She knew he was gone. She lay for a long time, her cheek pressed to the grass. Finally her sobbing became less intense. Her tears diminished as did the night and gray morning crept over the prairie.

The rude cross stood out then and the girl arose and walked to the fresh mound of soil nearby. The cross was of thronga—two yellow branches fastened with a strip of bark.

Kay sank to her knees. There was no inscription, but she knew. Cory had been there before her. He had buried his dead and he was gone.

"Cory…Cory…Cory…" But no longer a call. Only a cry and a prayer.

CHAPTER TWELVE

NATE GOODROW'S place lay along the north bank of the fourth canal. A pleasant, rectangular stretch of country rich in farming possibilities. But he'd never gotten the place lined up to suit him. There was always something to be done—something he couldn't entrust to anyone else. And later with things running smoothly he found, to his surprise, that the wanderlust had been drained from his blood. Oh, it was still there, but in such a mild degree that the trouble of getting started north didn't seem worthwhile.

He thought often of the people he'd known up above. He thought often of the Balleaus. They should be doing pretty well by now, he opined. That boy Cory, and odd one for sure, that lad. There was probably a freight head in Ngania by now. Nate was sure glad John Balleau had been able to wait out the bad times. He'd have to hit north one of these days and find out how the Balleaus were getting along. Damned if he wouldn't. Maybe he could talk Cory into coming down to the place for a season. The boy stayed too close to home and that was certain. Get him out here and let him ride the country for a couple of months and mix with the boys and he'd come out of himself. He was like a turtle in a shell, that boy.

Course he'd had some pretty rugged times. That fight back on the Marsport River for instance. No eleven-year-old should ever see a thing like that. Then his mom dying the same night. Pretty rugged on a youngster. But John Balleau had done a good job raising the lad. A lot of young ones without parents drifted into lawlessness and that was the end of them. They were just gallows-bait then, set to die when a posse out-guessed them.

Yeah, John Balleau had done a good job.

It was morning and Nate had just roped a *goff* and was swinging the saddle up when he saw three riders approaching from the northeast. They were coming slowly and riding close together. Nate studied them, watching them grow larger. Then it appeared that two of them were his own boys. Jimmy Clare and Lew Sackey. That was all right. They were about due in, but who was the other one?

Lean as a fence post he was, and riding a *goff* that was all bones and neck. Rode funny too, like he was sick or something. Kind of familiar though. Kind of—

Nate Goodrow was in the saddle, pounding out to meet the trio. He jerked off his hat, started to wave it as a cry of welcome arose to his lips. But he put the hat back on his head and the yell was never uttered. Something wrong. The way that boy rode. The way he looked! What in all hell? Nate skidded his mount to a stop and spun the beast around on its hind legs.

"Cory! As I live and breath it's Cory Balleau. Welcome boy!"

THE WAN face smiled and the smile could have been one of gratitude. "Hello Nate. I remembered that you invited me down here once. Glad it still holds."

"You're a sight for sore eyes, lad," Nate said. He caught himself but not quickly enough because Cory smiled bitterly.

"I sure must be a sight. I'll admit that," said Cory.

"I meant you're welcome to spend the rest of your days here. How's your uncle?"

When Cory ignored the question Nate didn't press it. He swung in beside them and the small talk back to the house was almost painful.

"The boys'll take care of the animals," Nate said at the gate. "I'll see about rousting you up a steak about four inches thick."

Cory slid from his *goff*. "Thanks but they fed me already. If it's all the same to you I'll hit the tank for maybe twelve or fourteen hours. I'm done in."

"Sure—sure. Come on in the house. You can have a back room and shut the door and sleep for a year."

Nate Goodrow took his guest into the house. Ten minutes later he was back at the corral. The two men had finished with the *goff*s and were blowing like porpoises in the watering trough.

"Where'd you find him?" Nate asked.

Jimmy Clare blew water out of his nose and said, "He come up to Number Three cabin this morning—early. Woke me up. I opened the door and thought I was seein' a walkin' ghost. He said he was hunting for you and could I tell him where your place was. I told him he was standing on it. Said he knew you up north and had an invite. We gave him some grub and when Torky showed, we brought the kid on in."

"Did he talk? Did he say anything?"

Sackey said, "Not much. Nothing at all about how he got beat to all hell and gone. Looks to me he must have been jumped by a gang, but he didn't say nothing about that. Said he'd been riding practically day and night though, and from the looks of his *goff* he ain't lying much."

Nate rubbed at his bristly chin and walked slowly away. Had the kid been attacked on the way down? If he wasn't going to talk, Nate was sure going to spend some time wondering. But there was something else. Nate had asked about John Balleau and Cory hadn't answered. Was the boy just too tired to hear? Nate frowned over that one. He'd just have to wait a few hours to find out, that was all.

Goodrow went vaguely about his business.

When Cory awoke the house was dead still. The darkness told him that it was night. He wondered what time it was. He could have gone right back to sleep, but he was possessed of a terrible thirst. He got up and pulled on his pants and boots. He went softly through the house so as not to waken Goodrow, and out the back door.

A voice asked, "Feeling better son?"

It was Nate's voice and the smell was from Nate's pipe. The pipe glowed in the darkness.

"Yes, a lot better. I thought you were asleep."

"I waited around. Figured you might perk up and maybe be hungry."

"No—just thirsty. What time is it?"

"Little after midnight. I'll walk out to the windmill with you."

THEY STRODE along in silence until Nate said, "I asked about your uncle this morning but you were pretty tired. Guess you didn't hear me."

"I heard you."

"You must not have felt like answering then."

"No. I guess I didn't. Uncle John is dead."

"I'm right sorry to hear that, son."

"He was killed by a deputy marshal named Dorken— Mel Dorken—when they came to take our land."

"You mean you lost your farm?"

"We lost it. Some kind of a fast shuffle on a loan. I don't know what it was all about, but when they came,

Uncle John got out the rifle. They shot him and he bled to death."

The windmill was turning slowly bringing a small stream of clear cold water into the storage tank. Nate slipped a valve handle and the water shot out into the *goff* trough. Cory drank thirstily from a tin cup.

Nate dragged on his pipe. "Mel Dorken, eh?"

"You know him?"

"Know *of* him. Hardly on speaking terms though."

"Sure—you'd know who he is. He blinded a man in a fight back on the Marsport. I saw it."

Nate's voice sharpened. "You remembered him from that fight?"

"As soon as I saw him in a Ngania drinking hall one day."

"Hmmm."

Cory put down the dipper.

Nate said, casually. "I've been thinking of taking me a little trip north. Been needing a change."

"Nate."

"Yeah?"

"I don't want it that way."

"What way?"

"I've got to fight my own battles. I've got to kill that man Dorken."

"Well—I'll admit he certainly needs killing."

"When I left Ngania I broke a store window and stole two pyro-guns, Nate. I came down here to ask you to teach me how to use them."

"You didn't have to steal guns, boy. We've got plenty."

"I know it, but somehow I had to steal those guns. Don't ask me why, because I don't know. And they're the guns I've got to use. Will you teach me?"

"A man should know how to defend himself. No reason why you shouldn't pick up a little gun knowledge. But I'm getting old and kind of stiff. Not what I used to be."

"If I get to be half as good as you are—I'll be satisfied."

"I could hold my own in a gun fight," Nate conceded, "but I never ranked with the best because I had one thing missing."

"What was that?"

"The love of a gun, boy. To rank with the top men you've got to have more than just skill and speed and even luck. You've got to love a gun and what it stands for. You've got to love to kill."

"The way Dorken loves it?" Cory asked with bitterness.

NATE KNOCKED the dead ashes from his pipe. "That's right, boy. You put two good men against each other and that's when a split second counts. A shade of an advantage, and the man who doesn't love to kill—who has an unconscious dread of seeing another man lose his life—won't get that advantage. The split second goes to the born killer and all the top gun slicks—owl-hooters and lawmen alike—have got that love."

"I'm living for just one thing, Nate—to kill Mel Dorken. If I couldn't look forward to that, there'd be just nothing. I'd have no future."

Nate sighed. "I hate to hear you say it, Cory. God knows you've got just cause, but I'd still rather hear you tell me you've walked away from it all and want to stay here and raise cattle with me and maybe someday own this place."

"And I wish I could say it, too—but I can't."

Nate dropped his arm around the boy's shoulder. When he spoke his tone was brisk. "Come on back to the house. I'll bet you can use some more sleep. Let's get you back on your feet. Then we'll talk about guns."

Cory offered no explanation for his battered face and the sprawling purple bruise on his throat. Nor did Nate Goodrow make inquiries. He noticed that Cory winced under certain bodily movements. He thought: *The lad was beaten up—beaten bad. I wonder if that was Mel Dorken's work too?* But it never occurred to him to make blunt inquiries.

Cory—for well over a month—conducted himself as though he had not a care in the world. He lounged in the sun, rode the range and finally began swimming in the Canal. He took long trips, got acquainted with Nate's men. His bruises faded swiftly. Within a month there was only a faintly dark area on his throat and his wiry body was free of aches and tender spots.

It was then that he brought out the two pyro-guns. Nate found him one day, seated on the back porch, cleaning and oiling the weapons.

"No change in your ideas, eh son?"

Cory shook his head briefly. He said, "Nate—I've got a little money—not much—and these damn things need ammunition."

Nate scratched his chin. "You know where the gun room is. There's enough gun-food in there to stand off the Venusian army for six months. And don't be talkin' about money. The stuff ain't much good down on these parts."

"Thanks."

"Hook 'em on, son."

Cory got up and slid the guns into their leather. He hefted the pellet belt, put it around his middle and fastened the catch. Nate eyed him, moodily and said, "You know what you're doing, don't you, boy?" Cory looked up sharply and Nate went on, "With what you got in your mind, you just put on something that's got to be closer than your underwear. From now on those guns will be pounding your legs at every step. Wherever you leave those guns you leave your life. Think the whole thing's worth it?"

CORY SLID his hands over the steel and purple leather. He looked down at the ungainly bulges on his thighs.

"There's no other way," he said.

Nate retained his somber expression. He took twenty pellets from his own belt and poured them into Cory's hand.

"Load 'em up."

Cory broke one of the guns and fumbled pellets into holder. One dropped to the ground.

"There's so much to learn," Nate said, "and while your at it there's no use skipping any. Now you take loading a gun. Nobody pays much attention to that but a fast load might save your life sometime. Get so you can do this."

Nate pulled his gun and dumped the pellets into his palm. He shook them around for a moment and they lay in a line—lead forward—along a groove formed by his palm and fingers. He then tilted his hand over the holder of his gun and moved the hand in a circular motion.

"See? Just like little trained pigs."

The pellets dropped swiftly into the cylinder and Nate snapped the gun shut. "You can load that way in fifteen seconds. Let's see how you can shoot..."

Cory raised the two weapons—held them tilted skyward; he squinted toward the fence, selecting a post.

"Just use one. This two-gun stuff is way over-rated. No man alive can hit two different targets at the same time and no man can draw two guns as fast as he can draw one. Except as a spare, that iron on your left leg is so much added weight."

Obediently, Cory put the left gun away and fired three times at a fence post with the right one.

One side of the post was faintly seared.

"Missed by two feet. A natural squeeze pulls your shot to the left." Nate faced the post and his right hand moved downward toward his leg—a smooth easy sweep of his arm. His fingers caressed leather and the gun was in his hand. The movement continued on in a backward arc. Nate's wrist bent at an angle that leveled his weapon. The whine came just as the tip of the barrel cleared the leather—while his arm was still moving backward. The top half of the thronga post disappeared, and without breaking the sweep of his arm movement, Nate reversed the arc and the gun went back into the clip. The whole operation was completed as a single unit: draw, fire, return—a beautifully integrated muscular coordination that took approximately one second to complete.

"That's not a fast draw," Nate said. "I'm way out of practice and when I was in practice I wasn't too fast. Facing a top gun-slick, I'd have been dead before my hand hit the butt. That's a draw that will do for rattlesnakes and killing broken-legged animals but that's about all. And if you're too close to the rattler he'll even beat you."

Cory stared morosely at the post.

"A draw isn't your problem though, son. You've got to learn to hit what you're shooting at first. You start out with fence posts and you end up by tossing pebbles in the air. When you can hit the pebble, you can feel that your aim won't let you down. Then start worrying about a fast pull."

"There's a lot to learn all right," Cory said.

"AND REMEMBER this, son. There's no such thing as the 'fastest gunman.' That critter just doesn't exist. But the woods are full of gun-slicks that are faster than each other, if you get what I mean."

"I think I do."

"Guns are strange things and it all adds up to this: No matter how swift you are—there's a man somewhere that's able to shoot quicker and, just as sure as fate, you're going to meet him. Always remember that."

"I'll remember."

Time went on, and Nate found himself to be strangely disturbed at the tenacity with which Cory worked—the deadly intent that was mirrored there in his eyes. If Nate had had any hope of the youth cooling down and abandoning his mania, that hope died as Cory pursued his dogged way.

The whine of the pyro-guns had grown so commonplace that even the animals in the corral no longer raised their heads or pricked up their ears.

Cory set up a target range behind the bunkhouse and slammed away at it with dogged persistence. When any of the hands used the day for sleep, he rode off toward the river.

Nate made the decision to leave the boy pretty much to himself. Though viewing Cory's ambition with a definite degree of sadness and misgiving, Nate would nonetheless have been willing to help—and *was* willing at any given time. But he sensed that Cory preferred to work out certain things for himself. Not that he didn't accept the advice Nate gave—accept it most gratefully—but Nate sensed a drawing back, a desire for privacy, and the ex-scout did not intrude.

Cory could hit a pebble tossed into the air, now. He wore the two guns, but he used only one.

ANOTHER change was perceptible to Nate Goodrow. The youth was becoming surer of himself. The change was apparent in his walk, in all his movements, and in his conversation.

And Nate had to admit that, from all outward appearances, here was a killer.

Cory's stride was a lithe motion of his entire body. He carried himself seemingly on tiptoe at an times, his shoulders sloping downward at a much more pronounced angle. There was even a certain follow-through in every motion he made that was the result of natural coordination not found in one man in a thousand.

The whine of the guns increased in tempo, as time went by, week after week. Then one day Cory came to Nate Goodrow and said, "Show me how to use a knife the way you do."

Here Goodrow noted another definite change. Six months back Cory would have put it differently. Something like: "You can sure throw that knife. I wonder if maybe you'd show me how?"

Now it was more like an order, spoken with cold assurance:

"Show me how to use a knife the way you do."

Nate said, "All right son. You take it this way…"

Nate was glad he'd had so little to do with it. Glad now, as he contemplated this newly created lethal masterpiece.

Cory had turned into the sort of lethal machine Nate didn't care to contemplate.

"He's yet to kill a man, though," Nate said. "That's the test. He's yet to kill a man."

CHAPTER THIRTEEN

CORY BALLEAU killed a man the following week.
He'd ridden, with a couple of Nate's men into the
settlement to pick up some supplies for his trip north.
They arrived there at around ten in the morning and the
two men were ready to leave by four in the afternoon.

But Cory had gotten a few credits ahead in a card game
at the local drinking hall. He showed no inclination to
leave, so his companions went on their way back to the
spread.

Early in the evening, the game got a new customer. A
wiry, dark-faced man who made frequent trips to the bar
during the play. Liquor loosened his tongue. He lost
money with jovial abandon. His laugh was grating and it
annoyed Cory. Cory ignored the man, however, until the
latter said, "Haven't seen you around here before, son.
Where you from?"

Every eye at the table centered on the man. This was
unthinkable. Even liquor scarcely excused a man from
committing a breach of etiquette so monstrous. However,
Cory saw nothing out of the ordinary in the inquiry.

"Ngania," he said, "'Up North."

The other slapped a palm on the table. "Well cut me
off short... I got a friend up that way. A man named
Dorken, Mel Dorken. Know him?"

The soles of Cory's boots pressed hard against the floor.
He studied his cards with elaborate attention. Finally he
said, "I know him."

"Me—I'm Deac Thomas, pardner," The man waited.

"Cory Balleau."

"Well it's a damn small globe. I'll take two. Make 'em queens. Heard from a man that rode down not long ago. Mel's doin' pretty good. Damn town's boomin' now, with a freight head in there, and Mel's a deputy marshal."

Thomas threw back his head and roared with laughter. "A deputy marshal. If that ain't one to hoot over!"

"So the freight head finally got there?"

Thomas got up and went to the bar. He downed two straight shots of whisky, wiped a hand across his mouth and came back to the table; he threw in his ante and roared again.

"Yeah, old Mel and me sure had some high times together. Knew him back when he was a mechanic working the truck trains. Great pal to have sidin' you—Mel. He liked his women plumb raw!"

Cory threw in his hand and got up from the table. There was an odd, cold feeling in the pit of his stomach. He went to the bar and ordered a schooner of beer. Maybe that would warm up the cold place. He sipped at the stuff. It was bitter and strong and it didn't help. He stood there until Thomas lumbered across the floor and stood beside him.

THOMAS' hilarity was fading. The look of amiability had departed from his face. He poured himself three fingers.

"You ain't said much, Balleau. You act almost as if you don't like my friends."

The man had reached the belligerent stage. He was spoiling for trouble and a certain tension filled the place. The game went on, the players appearing to give their cards more study—deeper attention.

Cory was silent.

Thomas scowled. "You know Mel Dorken, or don't you?"

"I know him."

Thomas considered that, tossed off his drink. "Maybe you had a brush with him or somethin' like that?"

"Maybe I did."

"Talk up! For cryin' out loud…look at a man when you're speakin' to him!"

Cory turned his head and spoke straight into Thomas' teeth. "Dorken's a yellow-bellied rat! You can smell him a mile away."

Thomas swung an arm, backhand. He hit Cory's shoulder, spinning the youth away from the bar. Cory staggered a few steps, got his balance and straightened. Thomas was facing him, ugliness paramount in his face.

"Nobody talks about my friends like that!"

Had Nate Goodrow been present, he would have told himself: This is it. This is the test. A man can learn everything there is to know about guns and gun fighting. But until he kills a man he's not a killer.

Cory stared at Thomas and thought: *You're inviting this. This is what you've been wanting ever since the liquor hit you cross ways. You've got to kill somebody and you picked me. You want it this way.*

And there was a quick feeling of elation in Cory's heart. And no fear. Fear was so far away that it did not penetrate his mind even as an abstract thought.

Cory said, "I don't want to kill you, man." But he lied. He lied and he knew he was lying. He wanted nothing in the world so much as to test his skill against Deac Thomas.

Thomas grew dark in the face. "Why you spindlin' little maverick!"

Cory watched him with the cold detachment of an iced mountain peak. With sure instinct he looked at Thomas with unfocused eyes—eyes that took in the whole of the man—no particular part of him. Thus the slightest movement of any part of Thomas' body would register instantly.

The killer's stare.

Thomas went for his gun and Cory cut him down in his tracks. He burned the man down to his belt before his gun was half out of its holster.

Thomas never had a chance.

Cory holstered his right hand gun, stepped over Thomas and picked up the beer schooner. He drained it, then turned and walked out of the saloon. He mounted his *goff* and rode slowly out of town.

It was night and the darkness was comforting in that it matched the mood of Cory Balleau. The soft clop-clop of his mount was a restful rhythm.

Coldly the youth searched his mind—examined his emotions, for any change, any newness born of an act he had never before indulged. There was no change whatever.

He had just killed a man and it seemed the most natural thing in the world for him to do. It was as if he had been killing men all his life. He was neither elated nor depressed; there was within him only a desire for solitude—the solitude of the night. And, oddly, he was tired, as though he had just completed a full day's work.

He smiled grimly. Evidently killing a man was a job of work in itself.

NATE GOODROW was sitting on bench by the back door when Cory rode up. The bowl of Nate's pipe glowed cherry-red.

Cory disposed of his *goff* and came across the back yard. He dropped down on the bench beside Nate. "The freight head finally got there," he said.

"You heard?"

"Met a man. He heard."

"It's sure a shame your uncle couldn't—had to be—"

"I know. It was a shame. This man's name was Thomas. Know anything about him?"

"Not much. Hasn't got too good a record."

"He knew Mel Dorken."

"Dorken was one of them too. Nobody on Terra felt bad when Frake and Snead and Dorken came to Mars."

"Snead was killed."

"That so?"

"Some night riders took him out and hung him."

"He was a slippery little cuss. Ain't at all surprised to hear he finished up at the end of a rope."

"They never caught the lynchers—or not before I left anyhow."

"Pretty hard to tie a kill on men like that."

There was a time of silence. Nate drew calmly on his pipe. Cory kicked at the dark earth with a boot-toe.

"You've been awfully good to me," Cory said. "I appreciate it."

Nate took his time before answering; "Ain't no call to bring that up, son."

"I wanted you to know that I appreciate it."

"Anytime. Anytime, son."

An empty spot.

"I'm heading north tomorrow."

"Thought you'd start getting restless. Better take that big black. He's got the weight for long hauls and I ain't seen anything faster for quite a spell."

"Thanks."

"No need to thank me."

Cory stood up, stretched himself, taking all the time needed to do it well.

"Guess I'll turn in."

"Good idea. You'll need sleep."

"Goodnight."

"Goodnight, son. Guess I'll sit a while."

THE SOUND of Cory's boots diminished into the house. Then he turned, came back and stood by the bench.

"Nate."

"Yeah?"

"That man, Thomas. I killed him."

"Kind of figured you did."

"How did you know?"

"Oh, a hunch maybe. And the way you talked about him—in the past as though he wasn't with us any more."

"I beat him on the draw."

"You better head out before dawn. Travel fast and get out of the Canal country."

"But it was fair. He reached first."

"He may have been among friends. You can't tell what they'll say about it."

"That's right."

Cory went to bed and lay open-eyed, staring at the ceiling. He was rested now. There wasn't a bit of weariness in him. Sleep was miles away.

But it came swiftly. Within three minutes his eyes were closed and he was breathing evenly.

NGANIA HAD had become a boomtown. With the coming of the big ships the place hitched up its tattered pants and let out a whoop-hooray that was heard far across the prairie.

Lumber was now plentiful and the town expanded. Paint, plastic and cement became the order of the day, and land hungry Terrans flocked in, their eyes on the soil.

Frank Bates had moved up several rungs toward the goal of his ambitions. He had come to think of himself as the biggest man in the community—had grown used to the idea—had become a little more hard-faced and far more rapacious.

He was hated and feared, now, but that made little difference to him. In fact the sense of power over his fellow men had, for him, a heady taste. The black squares in his map stretched in all directions, and he spent a great deal of time brooding over the squares that still remained white.

He had become the man to whom the people looked for leadership in spite of the fact that he was unpopular. Frank Bates' opinion was solicited on all-important matters and that opinion had a way of becoming the majority opinion.

His relationship with Frake was a great deal more vague than anyone suspected; vague in the sense of a definite understanding. Frake, as Marshal of Ngania, ran the town, but he was careful to run it as Bates wished. And Frake was willing to ride along and bide his time. He drew his salary and accepted a certain amount of graft where it could be gotten, but he was careful not to overplay his hand. The man had an instinct for staying out of obvious trouble. Eventually he would make his killing and he was entirely willing to let events shape themselves without forcing them.

Times were on the upsweep. He was content to watch.

CHAPTER FOURTEEN

CORY Balleau rode into Ngania, paused at the lower end of town. He lounged there in the saddle, totally unaware of how close upon the heels of his destiny he was treading.

It had grown. It wasn't the same town he'd left—Ngania. There were more people. The main street was transformed. This was something to stare at—something to get used to.

Cory touched the *goff's* flank and moved on. There was the gunsmith's shop. The window he'd smashed to steal the two guns was gone. A larger one had taken its place and there were more guns inside.

There were more guns outside too. Almost every male right hip was sporting a gun. The town had changed.

Well, I've changed too, Cory thought. That made it even.

He dismounted in front of the Golden King and surveyed the new plastic front. There was a look of prosperity here. Cory climbed the three stairs to door-level and pushed the door.

There wasn't much change inside. Only a new and longer mirror behind the bar. There was also a new bar-keep, a fat, apron-wearing man who came down the bar and stood in front of Cory and did not recognize him.

Cory ordered beer. The schooners hadn't diminished in size and Cory leaned against the bar feeling the beer run cold into his stomach.

He was inspected covertly by the three or four other drinkers at the mahogany. They eyed his two guns and seemed to be trying to reconcile them with Cory's entirely apparent youth.

Rearward a poker game was going on at the old table. Cory had spotted Frake sitting in on this game; spotted him immediately upon entering. He watched Frake with a sense of disappointment. He had hoped to find someone else in the Golden King; someone who looked a great deal like the Marshal but who went under another name.

Mel Dorken.

BUT DORKEN was conspicuously among the absent. Cory finished his beer and set down the schooner. It was the sound of the glass hitting the bar that brought Frake's head up. Frake glanced idly forward and his eyes drifted back to his cards. Then his head came up sharply.

Cory Balleau...

Why what the hell? John Balleau's nephew was back. The kid had a cock-eyed crust if Frake ever saw one. Frake scowled and got to his feet.

He moved forward with decisive strides, thumbs hooked in his pellet belt. He walked straight toward Cory. When he spoke his voice was hostile.

"Kind of nervy, coming back to this town, ain't you?"

There was genuine surprise in Cory's face. "Why? What's nervy about coming back to my home town?"

"Well, for one thing a couple of guns were stolen the night you left. Somebody smashed a window and pulled them right out of a store. They were just like the ones you're wearing. That's why I say you've got kind of a nerve."

Cory made no answer. He stepped casually away from the bar and faced Frake.

Frake said, "I think you and I better walk over to my office and have a little talk about those guns."

"We don't walk anywhere—together," Cory said.

"Now look here, son—"

Frake was curious about the boy—that odd motion of his. Almost a girlish motion wherein Cory raised his left arm from the elbow held rather close against his side. The hand was open, flat—stiff—with the palm out. It was sort of a salute, that motion, or rather like a girl getting ready to give a playful slap.

"If you take me anywhere, you take me with your gun, and I wouldn't reach for that if I were you."

Surprise and indignation. A scowl, and Frake said, "Why you damned little—" He reached for his gun.

Cory charred him down.

Cory holstered his right-hand gun and backed toward the door, his left hand up in the mock salute. No word was said. The witnesses, both Terrans and Martians, could have been stone men. They stood frozen.

They heard the pound of *goff* hooves from the street. The sounds faded.

CORY BALLEAU rode out of Ngania, and the thought of pursuit was not foremost in his mind. Mainly, he considered the frustration of the incident in the Golden King. He had killed the wrong man, and the emotion engendered by so doing was one of irritation. Why couldn't he have been more fortunate? He had come to Ngania with one purpose—to kill Mel Dorken. Now, because of an unfortunate accident, the difficulty of his enterprise would be multiplied. Now there, would be a manhunt. Posses would scour the country. Cory Balleau was a marked man. Reaching Dorken, now, would be a problem.

It was only at this point that Cory realized the direction in which he was traveling—a clear path, straight across country toward the old place. This was pure foolishness. He should be heading west, into the rocky country where he could find sanctuary and get his bearings. This way, they would be on his heels in no time.

But the nostalgia within him—the urge for just a fleeting look at the house and the pond and the clean fields—won out, and he kept on going. There was the creek, a bright green line on the prairie; off to the left, the grove where he'd lain in the grass and Kay's golden hair...

He thought of her for the first time in weeks. Even upon arriving in Ngania, his mind had found no time to give her even a moment. His grim face softened a trifle now. Had she forgotten him? Probably. She was young and, regardless of the previous attachment, she would forget quickly, he thought. He rambled thus, without the slightest realization that, at twenty-two, he had excluded himself from the category of youth. She was a nice girl. He granted this, wished momentarily and vaguely that things could have worked out differently, and then forgot her.

There it was. He reined up and stared, straightening, standing erect in the stirrups.

The place was deserted. Evidently Frank Bates had been too busy to give attention to his new property. Or perhaps there were technicalities created by the death of John Balleau.

It occurred to Cory, that, even now, he himself could be there working the homestead, carrying on in his uncle's place. He could have gotten the money from Nate Goodrow to payoff the loan. He thought of this not as an opportunity overlooked, but as merely a curious point. Curious in the sense that such a course had never entered his mind until this moment.

He took in the scene before him, deserted, weed-grown, bleak even under the hot sun of an unclouded Martian sky.

He nudged the *goff* and moved forward. Then, glancing back, he immediately pulled up.

THEY WERE already on his trail three riders a mile rearward, coming at a gallop directly toward him. Cory felt only a sense of irritation. He had expected them and it was no surprise, but couldn't they have given him a few more minutes? He swung off course, westward, and went into a dead run. He wasn't greatly worried. He knew of a place among the rocks over in the ridges where he could stand a posse off all day. Only three men. He could no doubt get one of them, or even two. Then, in the darkness, he could slide out.

The three riders pulled up as Cory started his westward run. They seemed to be in conference. Then they veered their own course and came on.

Oddly, they made no attempt to cut him off. That might not have been possible, but it was certainly worth a try. Cory wondered. And only three of them. That was hardly a posse to send after a man who had just gunned down the marshal. Odd indeed. Cory traveled on, hugging the course of Cotter's Creek, following it until twisted away to the south.

The three men did likewise—holding their distance, even shortening it somewhat.

Cory studied the situation. Then he pulled the *goff* into a slower gait and hauled a para-rifle out of its boot. The rifle was loaded and ready and it seemed worth while to risk a brush with the three riders. If they dared come close enough, there would speedily be only two of them. Two, Cory felt, was better than three. And possibly Dorken…

The *goff* traveled at a canter now, and the three riders came on. Half a mile…a quarter… Cory pulled his mount to a walk. Closer now and he could see that Dorken was not one of the three. The *goff* came to a halt as Cory decided on a try at four hundred yards.

He dismounted and went flat on the ground, cuddling the para-rifle stock against his cheek. The lead man came into his sights.

But the men were acting strangely. They were all afoot now. As Cory watched, they unbuckled their side arms and threw them in a pile on the ground. Then one of them yelled something unintelligible and started walking forward. His hands were in the air.

He came silently forward. At a hundred yards, Cory shunted the rifle barrel upward and called, "That's far enough."

The man replied, "We want to talk, my Terran friend. We're not after you. We're friends…"

"Hold your distance. I haven't got any friends in these parts."

"If you're the man that burned Frake down, you've got three of them, mister. We come to throw in with you."

Cory considered this. He had never seen any of these men before. This could be a trick, but if so, it was a far riskier one than the three realized. Cory bit at his lower lip, thoughtfully, then called, "All right. Walk up, but keep your hands high."

The man trudged forward. He was slight of build, hollow-cheeked. He had large blue eyes, eyes tending to bulge.

HE STOPPED at twenty feet when Cory said, "Your friends back there. Tell them to face the other way. Then I won't have to watch them so close."

The man grinned. He turned and began waving, making circular motions with his hands. Finally the two men got the drift and stood facing away. They lowered their arms and stood with thumbs hooked in their belts.

"You wouldn't be trying to hold me here would you?" Cory asked.

"What for?"

"A posse maybe—coming on behind."

"Nothing like that. You're John Balleau's son aren't you? Cory Balleau?"

"That's right."

"Knew your uncle. Knew him pretty well from meeting him in Ngania. Name's Jim Kendall."

"I never went to town much."

"No. I never seen you there and I guess you never saw me. But you heard of something I had a hand in."

"What was that?"

"Hanging Tip Snead."

"You—lynched Tip Snead?"

"Not lynch, son. We executed him. We gave him the same as he gave Sam Bendorf."

"You and who else?"

"There was five of us. We all lost our land to Frank Bates. Two pulled out—they had wives and kids, but I'm still here and that's Mike Taber and Paul Thompson back there."

"Why did you follow me?"

"To throw in with you. It was luck, mainly, that got us out of town before the posse. Thompson was in the drinking hall and saw you kill Frake. We was hanging around town and so we lit out after you."

Cory's expression mirrored uncertainty. He studied the man. There were other things too. Did he want these men to side with him? Had he—any need of allies?

"Look, Balleau," Kendall said. "You better make up your mind quickly. We aren't wishing you any harm and standing around out here could be a little dangerous—for all of us maybe. They're getting a posse together and it's probably on its way now and you left a trail a blind man could follow. If you don't want us, say the word and we'll be on our way."

Cory made his decision with characteristic swiftness and certainty. Once made, it was done and finished. No backward glance.

"Tell them to come on and let's get going."

Kendall yelled and waved, whereupon his companions gathered up their gear and remounted. They came forward at a gallop. As Cory watched them, his thought was the logical one for his single-track mind to produce.

I wonder if this will get me within shooting distance of Mel Dorken any quicker?

CHAPTER FIFTEEN

THEY KNEW of a comparatively isolated stop in the rocky country further west. An optimistic squatter had come and gone and there was a sod lean-to against an eighteen-foot wall with a corral further in and a narrow exit out into the boulders a half-mile back.

There was bacon and Martian sardo beans from Cory's pack and Mike Taber did the cooking. Paul Thompson was bigger than the other two combined. He seemed darker than even sunburn could make him, and looked much more foreign than his name. After eating, he went to the mouth of the canyon and sat down on a rock, taking over watch duty without a word.

The remaining three sat on the dark ground and put their backs against the sod wall.

"You're a funny one," Kendall said to Cory. "I can't make you out, Balleau."

"Why funny?"

"I don't know. It's like you don't realize what you did, or something—like you've got no nerves maybe. You rode into Ngania and pulled your pyro-gun and shot the town marshal! You realize that?"

"I shot the wrong man."

"Who were you gunning for?"

"Mel Dorken. He's the one I came north to kill."

Taber scratched his chin. "He was the one that shot your uncle. Anyway that's how it got noised around. Self-defense."

"Uh-huh. I shot Frake in self-defense too," Cory said with bitterness.

Kendall turned his head and eyed Cory with speculation. "You aiming to stick around until you get a crack at Dorken?"

"I'm going to kill him."

"Seems to me you went about it in a bad way. Before, you could have walked up and done it anytime. Now maybe it could be a bit harder to get close enough."

"I'll figure out a way."

Kendall sat silent, mulling something over in his mind, and Cory said, "That lynching. You men moved awfully fast. What was behind it? What did you expect to gain?"

Kendall's eyes narrowed. "What do you expect to gain by killing Dorken?"

Cory thought for a moment. "Yes. I see what you mean."

"We were all in the same boat. We'd been done out of our land by Bates and we all knew Bendorf well. It was only plain justice, and we figured we had to strike back. Guess we had a crazy idea to stir up some of the Terran settlers, too, but it didn't work out that way."

"Frake sure wanted to get his hands on you."

"And Bates too. He still does. That's why we were blocked on trying to stir up trouble for him. With that reward offered we had to keep our mouths shut. We were even worried about each other for a while. Then two of the boys moved on and us three kind of stuck together."

"Why did you want to hook up with me?"

This left Kendall a little at a loss. It was difficult for the man to explain why they'd instantly thought of Cory as being that leader. When driven to direct statement, it seemed absurd of Kendall, a forty-year-old man, to offer allegiance to a young man scarcely out of his teens.

He was never required to put it in words, however because, at that moment, Thompson called back from the mouth of the canyon, "Trouble coming! Straight up the line."

THE THREE by the cabin came to their feet. Kendall's face showed genuine surprise. "They track fast! Thought we'd be safe for the night."

At the gorge entrance they looked silently out at the trouble. A dozen riders a mile away, coming hard and fast.

"We've got to move," Cory said. "Head for your *goffs!*"

Immediately there was the whine of two para-rifles, a single sound, and five men rose up not a hundred yards due south. Thompson leaped back, cursing. He flung an arm across his eyes.

The four dived back into cover and Kendall yelled, "You hit, Paul?"

"Molten rock in the face."

"This is too open," Cory said. "We can't make a stand here. Back to the lean-to."

They ran silently. There was a hundred yards to cover before the attackers made the canyon mouth. Pellets were whining around the men's ears as they tumbled through the door.

Immediately Kendall was pushing the barrel of a para-rifle out the window.

"Don't use that," Cory said, sharply.

Kendall turned, questioning silently.

"You could only get one or two at the most," Cory said. "Maybe they'll get cocky and try moving in before the others get here. We've got to get them all—the whole five—or we're rats in a trap."

Thompson was shaking his head. The man seemed dazed, completely off balance. "I didn't see that first bunch. They must of come up out of the ground."

"They circled and worked back down country. They must have spotted us from across the prairie. Maybe they've got a tele-glass and saw us come in here."

"No wonder the posse was coming straight as a string," Kendall said. He was peering out the window and he saw that Cory was correct about the necessity of killing the five men. It had to be done before the main body arrived. This because the five, with rifles, covered the open area between the lean-to and the *goffs*. "Maybe they'll get within range if we stay quiet. Then we shoot and we don't miss."

Taber was calmly lifting pellets from his belt and putting them in a pile near the door. When he had a respectable heap, he sat down cross-legged and awaited developments. So far he had not spoken a word.

Outside, the five invaders showed signs of exuberance. There were yells echoing up the canyon. Already the men were celebrating a victory.

Cory watched as two of them came cautiously forward, moving close to the canyon wall. They evidently expected to draw fire. When none came they hesitated, held a short conference in low tones and waved the other three forward.

But only one of the three came further into the gorge to join the two. Cory frowned. They were playing it smart. Back near the entrance, two para-rifle barrels peered out from between rocks. The advance was going to be covered.

One of the advance guard yelled, "Come out you men! Crawl out with your hands up. We'll see you get a fair trial!"

"And a quick hanging," another of them bellowed. There followed a series of hearty guffaws. They were in high, good spirits.

CORY FINGERED his right-hand gun and studied the dark future. Not given to outbursts of anger, he nonetheless choked on quick rage as it welled up within him. Not rage at anyone or anything, but rather at the nebulous, mocking fate that was blocking him at every turn. Instead of getting closer to Dorken, he was coming closer to destruction. With plans laid for a safe hideout, he had to meet these three men and get himself maneuvered into a trap like this. His luck, definitely bad, had grown worse.

In a sudden spasm of frustration he dived for the door. He jumped into the open, landing, like a cat, on his toes. His left arm came around in a swift chopping motion, three times. Instantly the covering rifles whined a challenge. But Cory was back behind the shelter of foot-thick sod blocks, and Kendall was gaping through the window, lips hanging slack.

Kendall stiffened his mouth and muttered. "Great lord in heaven! What kind of shooting was that? The whole three—dead! Like they were cut down with a blow torch."

Then the approaching posse cavalcade arrived in a great clatter and sent a dust cloud lazing up the canyon. Now the entrance was alive with para-rifles. Glinting steel was poked out through cracks and from behind rocks. The trap was sprung.

"Damn!" Cory said, fervently. "We might have made it. I'm too slow. I'm just too damn slow!"

Cory surveyed the gorge entrance, standing well back from the door. He reached out a hand and picked up his rifle from where it leaned against the sod wall. Going down on one knee, he spotted a rather unwary gunman who had climbed to a vantagepoint four feet up the gorge wall. The man's head and shoulders were in plain sight. Cory lowered his sights on the bulging forehead and pressed the switch. The pellet went exactly where he sent it, and the man's lower torso came upward in agonized reflex and then tipped forward like a tree falling. He hit the canyon floor and flopped down like half a tired rag doll.

Kendall fired three times through the window, but he scored no hits. Then a positive hail of pellets drove the trapped men back from the window of the lean-to.

Cory sat on his heels in one corner and slid three pellets into his right-hand gun. He glanced out through the door and said, "We've got an hour of daylight left, and we've got to make a break before it's gone."

"That's suicide," Kendall said, mildly.

"Probably, but it's surer death to stay here after dark. There's no moon tonight and they'd just move in on us. If we wait until dark to slip out, we'll find them three feet from the door and they'd blast us to hell. We've got to run for it, one at a time."

"We won't make it though," Taber said. There was no fear, but rather a regretful sadness in his voice.

THOMPSON scowled. "Better than waiting for a sure pellet, though. He's right. We've got to break for it."

A silence filled the sod lean-to. It lasted only a few seconds, but it seemed like hours. Then Cory said, "Want to draw straws?"

"On who'll go first, you mean?" Kendall asked. He looked at the others. "Personally I'd just as soon have Balleau do the covering."

"The first man will have the best chance," Cory said. "The second and third, not so good. The fourth—" Cory shrugged. "He'll have no cover."

Simultaneously, both Kendall and Thompson looked at Taber. Taber caught their eyes and said, "I'm in no hurry."

"You get back there and have the *goffs* ready," Kendall said. "We'll all be along."

Taber peeled off his belt and Cory said, "You cover a hundred yards and you'll be all right. It will take a lot of luck to get you after that."

"I'll make it," Taber said.

Several men of the posse had moved up now. They had skirted the gorge walls and found shelter within easy range of the lean-to door. They kept up a desultory fire, but appeared to be waiting. In this, they were sensible. Why risk their lives when darkness would soon come to their aid?

Cory stepped to the window. He studied the layout before he said, "I'll take the close ones. Kendall, you use your rifle through the door and try to hold back their long-gun fire from back behind."

Kendall said nothing. He knelt down, slightly back from the doorway.

"I'll give you the word," Cory said.

He raised his guns, selected some targets, and said, "Jump!"

Mike Taber went out fast. He veered west, up the gorge, running low in a straight line.

Instantly Cory's guns began to bark. He switched the shots carefully. There was a scream from a posseman who had come to his feet to level a pyro-gun.

Kendall's rifle filled the lean-to with its whine, slugs spewing out as fast as he could eject empty shells.

Then Thompson, peering through the doorway at another angle, said, "He's down. They got him."

Cory and Kendall turned and saw Taber prone and motionless some forty yards up the canyon.

"I think I know who got him," Cory gritted. "Give me that rifle."

There were cheers from outside—sounds of savage elation—as Cory went flat on the ground inside the door. From behind a boulder, far back, he saw a lean figure come half-erect and lift his hat like an actor acknowledging applause.

"Was it you, Lane?" A voice yelled.

"My pellet," the man called back. "I want the bounty!"

There was laughter, punctuated by the whine of Cory's para-rifle and the lean figure stood perfectly still as the hat dropped out of sight behind the rock. There was a deathly pause and every eye watched the man pitch forward to hang over the big rock.

"Now!" Cory said. "Both of you! Run like hell! They're off guard!"

THE TWO reacted instantly. Thompson went lumbering out first, with Kendall in his wake, while Cory began pumping a deadly stream of pellets into the posse.

He was in no position to watch the progress of Thompson and Kendall. He kept on switching until his own gun was empty. Then he snatched up Kendall's and emptied that. He knew, with absolute certainty that he had killed nor hit no one, but he had kept many shots from following the two runners.

Now he moved around and looked up the canyon. Thompson was sprawled on the ground about twenty-five feet from the body of Taber. Kendall was not in sight.

"Kendall made it," Cory breathed. "The sons-of-bitches didn't get Kendall!"

Cory threw the rifle into a corner and saw Kendall's tobacco makings lying there on the floor. Cory seldom smoked, but now he squatted down and carefully rolled a cigarette. He lighted it with a match from his own pocket and drew the smoke into his lungs. It tasted good. He blew out a white cloud and watched the smoke curl, listening the while to shouts and comments from outside.

"Set us up another duck!" some one bellowed, and Cory thought: *I wonder where that one is? I'd like to kill him. I'd sure like to.*

Suddenly Cory felt the urge to yell. "Ten shots to hit a cigarette!" he bellowed. "Go home and get some practice!"

"It's Balleau! That's Cory Balleau!"

Cory felt loose and easy. "Who'd you think it was? Some waddy who handles a gun like you do?"

There was laughter and now an atmosphere of mock hilarity, but with a deadly undertone.

"We've heard some about your shooting, Balleau! I'll throw up a rock! See if can you hit it!"

Baiting the trapped animal.

"All right. Throw it."

A head and a hand appeared in the canyon—up from behind a dirt hummock. The hand tossed a pebble into the air.

Cory fired once, snapped the switch of his gun with, a quick chop of his left hand.

There was a gargled scream and the man who had tossed the pebble slapped both hands to a face that wasn't there and went over backwards.

"Missed," Cory yelled. "Damned if I didn't miss! What do you know about that?"

There was a concerted howl of rage against which Cory laughed as he got to his feet. He felt good. In all his life he had never felt so lighthearted and happy.

What am I doing in here, he thought. *I'm going out—now. Nobody's going to stop me.*

WITH THE sun low, he stepped out into the open and fired three shots.

"It's Cory Ball—" The man who shouted died with the rest of the name unspoken.

Cory's second pellet burned down another gunman, bringing him into the open, no longer caring about cover. The third melted rock and drove a third gunman down.

Cory turned and ran. He ran on his toes, light-footed, feeling like a cloud. The pellets singing around him were of no consequence. He made fifty yards and glanced back.

They we're up now—all of them up and silent and desperately shooting. Cory killed two of them with four shots—deadly pellets that either killed or missed entirely. Then he ran again, holstering his empty gun and moving the left one still in his right hand.

But he fired no more. He moved out of range, beyond the rocks, on flying feet, and there was Kendall holding two *goffs*, waiting.

"You made it," Kendall said. He could have been speaking of nice weather.

"My number's not up yet," Cory grinned, and they mounted and galloped up the canyon.

Cory thought: *I wonder if Dorken was there. Probably, but he sure kept under cover.*

Mel Dorken *was* with the posse. Acting town marshal now, he had to be there, but he saw no reason for risking his life, and directed operations from the rear.

He noted, with satisfaction, the deaths of Thompson and Taber. He'd always felt that they had been involved in Tip Snead's death and this proved it. Otherwise why would they tie up with an outlaw like Cory Balleau?

Elated with the way things were going, Dorken turned and looked back over the red prairie. He narrowed his eyes into the lowering sun. There was a rider approaching at a gallop and it was...

Damned if it wasn't! That yellow-haired girl he'd been obsessing over for months!

Dorken forgot the posse. He forgot that he was a Terran lawman. He forgot Cory Balleau and everything else but the desire to get that yellow hair in his hands.

And a plan to accomplish this didn't have to be formulated. It was there in his mind, instantly, as though it had been lying dormant, waiting to be put into action.

He turned to a man close by and said, "That's Bates' daughter coming. We don't want any women here. I'll head her off and get her back to her dad. Keep things going. I'll be back."

With that he mounted and rode off to meet the girl. He held his *goff* directly in her path, forcing her to rein up or swerve around him. She reined up and Dorken said, "It's too late to see anything. It's all over."

Kay Bates whitened. A hand went to her breast. She spoke two words, forming a question, "Cory—Balleau?"

Dorken exulted inwardly. He'd been right! Balleau was the reason for those trips she used to take into the country—out toward Cotter's Creek. She'd met the boy out there, and now that attachment dropped neatly into Dorken's plan.

CHAPTER SIXTEEN

WHEN A MAN changes as fast as Cory Balleau had changed, there are always lapses, recessions—if not of a physical skill, then of a mental nature. A reversion of some sort even if it takes only a mild form.

With Cory it was a quick wave of wonder sweeping through his consciousness. He was riding through the night beside Kendall—through the rocky country at the western edge of the farmland. He looked at the dim shadow beside him and said, "I killed at least four men back there and I've killed two others. A man should feel something after doing that—regret maybe, but I don't feel any different. I just feel sort of empty—like an old bucket."

"I guess that all depends on how it comes about—the killing I mean. Why did you come back to this town, son?"

"To get Mel Dorken."

"In other words you were just gunning for one man—not six or seven or whatever number got in your way."

"I guess that's right. But still I don't regret anything I've done. That's what bothers me. Shouldn't I at least feel a little sorry?"

Kendall's answer was a short, bitter laugh. "I don't know. I guess it's hardly any use worrying about it, though. I guess none of us had the cut of outlaws—you or I or Thompson or Taber. We just did what we thought we had to—to protect our own. Now Thompson and Taber are dead and here we are with a posse on our tails. Guess we didn't go about it right."

"I didn't see Dorken with the posse," Cory said.

Kendall was silent for a long minute. Then he said, "Cory, why don't you give up the idea—why don't you forget about killing Dorken?"

"Forget it?" Cory turned in his saddle to stare at Kendall.

"That's right. What's over is over. We were on the short end of the stick and whatever we did to get off was wrong for us. The proof of that is where we are now—can't push our heads over a rock without getting them burned off."

"I rode up here to kill Dorken."

"So you had a long ride. But what good's killing him going to do you? Haven't you killed enough men? Six is a pretty good record for the short time you've been in the business. Why not call it quits right now and we'll ride out of this region and start over. Maybe we can take a crack at durium mining down the South Canal way. Leave Dorken alone. Somebody'll get around to killing him before too long."

Cory rode in silence for a while. He glanced up into the nighttime sky and saw what appeared to be the light of a Terran spacecraft high overhead—probably headed for Marsport. It made him think back to his younger days when he had first come to Mars—of his mother and Uncle John. And now years later here he was, a fugitive riding across the Martian plains on a *goff* with a posse at his back.

For many months now he had thought of no future in which the killing of Dorken wasn't included. Yet he found himself open-minded enough to give such a future some serious consideration now that Kendall suggested it. But why so suddenly open-minded? He had turned a deaf ear to Nate Goodrow's warnings that the path he chose was a bleak and cheerless one. That had been such a short time ago. So whence had his present doubts sprung?

HE SAID, "Aren't you making a pretty sharp switch, Kendall? A few hours back you were all set for the outlaw trail. There wasn't anything left for any of us inside the law. Now you've changed your tune."

Kendall took some time before answering. He appeared to be seeking an answer to Cory's question. "I see your point, but a lot happened in that short time. Thompson and Taber are dead. There's been a battle, with other men killed. We've had a sample of what it's like and I don't think I've got the stomach for it."

Cory smiled grimly. "When you throw pellets they usually kill men."

"It's just that I can't see any use to it, and I have a feeling we're both in the same boat. Now take me, I did something—or helped do something—in the heat of anger that seemed just and right. It's a hard country out here and the law is slow in reaching it, so it looked as though we had the right to take it into our own hands."

He stopped and thought some more, then went on with greater surety: "But what has it got us—me? Am I better off for having done it? Have I got my place back? Am I a respected citizen? Snead's dead, but how did that help me? I'm running from a Terran posse now."

There was enough stark logic in Kendall's talk to make Cory uncomfortable.

"Your situation's the same only you haven't killed the man you're after yet. But you're in a pretty good spot to see what it's going to get you afterwards."

"I'm way out on the limb now," Cory said.

"I know how you're figuring," Kendall returned. "You think 'what's the difference?' One more man. What's another killing now more or less? But I've got a feeling, Cory, that it's damned important where you stop. Why don't you forget about Dorken and head out of here with me?"

They rode in silence, veering back into the prairie country. Cory should have been tired but he wasn't. Nor was there any inner demand for food.

"What you've really been trying to say," he observed, "is that you don't think either of us are natural outlaws."

"What I'm trying to say is that I hope it isn't too late. The law is after us now—sure—and it will stay after us, but it's what a man thinks of himself that counts. If we stop now we've got a certain justification for our past acts— small maybe, but a little comforting. You take out Dorken though, Cory, and you're a killer inside as well as out. There'll be no turning back then."

And now Cory was keenly aware of what had caused the uneasiness within him. He remembered the ease with which he had burned down those men. Almost with pleasure he had watched them fall lifeless—and that bothered him now. Did he enjoy killing? He *had* enjoyed it. Now he feared that sensation he had known, as drug addicts fear the white powder. He was suddenly afraid of himself as a killer.

"There's a limit to what a man can stand," Kendall said. "I'm about tapped out. Let's get a little sleep while the night holds and you can think over what I've said."

They roped out their mounts in a place where the grass touched their ankles and stretched out on the ground with their bedrolls for pillows. Kendall was asleep in three minutes, but Cory lay wide-eyed, looking up at the stars.

Oddly enough, he wasn't thinking of Mel Dorken. He thought of Kay Bates and there was the wish in him that her bright head could be close to him now, resting on his arm. He stared up at the stars for a long time. Then he sat up and called out to Kendall.

Kendall stirred and mumbled. Cory said, "How about the North Country? We can start at dawn. We can be out of this area in an hour—up in the rough country."

"Fine, son. Fine."

FRANK BATES rode the prairie alone in the darkness. He followed no particular route but cut a meandering trail that wound in a circle roughly northeast of Ngania.

At times he pulled his *goff* to a halt and called out, "Kay! Kay! Where are you? It's your father, Kay!"

But there was never an answer, and Frank Bates would ride on, knowing it to be foolish, but unable to do otherwise.

There was panic in his heart and a roiling of emotions that made him physically weak.

She had gone off at first word that the posse had Balleau trapped in the rocky gorge. Bates had followed later, to bring her back, to drag her if necessary, but she had already left.

They told him she'd left with Dorken. Dorken had felt that the canyon was no place for a girl and had said that he intended to see her home.

Bates' fear had been a small trickle of ice water through his mind when he'd heard that. Strange indeed that an Acting Town Marshal would leave important fugitives holed up in a canyon for any such reason as that.

Then, when Kay and Dorken failed to appear in Ngania, Bates went sick at the possibilities. Now he was wandering the prairie, unnerved by the appalling thing that he felt was happening.

Where was Kay? Where was Dorken?

So many things clarified for Bates now. These men he'd used to further his ends. Had he used them or were they using him? He'd always been somewhat afraid of Dorken, but with Frake to stand between, the danger had appeared small. He had seen Dorken looking at Kay more than once and had been annoyed. Now he realized that those looks had been far more sinister than he'd realized. Or had they?

Possibly his natural anxiety of the moment was magnifying his recollections. He rode on through the whispering grasses. At intervals he called out, "Kay! Kay! Where are you, Kay?"

CHAPTER SEVENTEEN

THE DECISION Cory made seemed to lift a cloud from his mind. He awoke just before dawn and was surprised at the eagerness with which he opened his eyes. There was a quickening, a sense of expectancy that warmed him. Somehow the world seemed new. He faced what lay ahead with an enthusiasm he hadn't known for a long, long time.

He watched the first faint signs of morning come out of the east, and when dawn broke he was on a nearby rise, checking for signs of water.

To the northwest lay dim ridges that were far higher than they seemed. Soon he would be crossing those mountains, moving toward a new life. The thought was pleasant.

Cory spotted a meandering creek a quarter of a mile northward, but no sign of life in any direction. He returned and got the *goffs* and took them to the creek. While they drank he stripped down and jumped into the icy water, rubbing himself down with clean sand.

Dressed again he returned to camp and found Kendall dressed. He had bacon frying over a small fire. When the meat was cooked, Kendall stamped out the fire and they wolfed the bacon down with old biscuits.

"We'll head straight for the Red Hills," Kendall said. "Then we can roam along on our own time. Maybe we'll hit something we like."

"I'd like to take a crack at durium mining," Cory said.

They were ready to go now and Cory pulled up at the top of the rise and twisted in the saddle. Kendall turned and rode back. "Aren't regretting your decision, are you?"

Cory shook his head. "Not for a second. I'd have liked to go back home once more though—just to look the old place over. I wonder what Bates will do with it."

"I heard he was going to build there himself. I think he swindled your uncle out of it. Frank Bates is a slick article. I don't think John Balleau would have signed a three-month note unless he was tricked into it."

Cory didn't answer. That was all over and done with now. Part of a past that was water over the fall. A past to be forgotten. And looking back toward the old place, Cory realized that the hardest part of it to forget would be Kay Bates. There was a definite longing when he thought of her. Too late now, though, he told himself.

He swung his *goff* toward the northwest and nudged it with a heel. Then he pulled up again and looked back. Kendall hadn't moved.

"A rider over yonder," Kendall said. "Maybe we overstayed our welcome."

Cory whirled back and they sat squinting southeast. The rider was over a mile away.

"Seems to be alone," Cory said, "and not coming toward us. Going straight north. Probably just some homesteader."

"We ought to get behind a hill maybe until he's out of sight."

"The hell with him. Let's get moving."

Still Kendall hesitated, his eyes squinted. "Something funny about that *goff*. It doesn't seem to be going anywhere. Look. It stopped to crop grass."

"You've got better eyes than I have," Cory said.

"They're pretty good all right," Kendall said.

"Let's cut across east on the other side of that rise," Cory said. "We can keep out of sight and get closer."

Kendall shook his head doubtfully. "It's damn foolishness, but come on, I'm kind of curious myself."

They rode east at an easy lope for their *goffs*, covered a half mile, and Kendall moved up to a vantagepoint.

"It's a—say! Damned if it isn't a girl!"

"What's a girl doing out here?"

CORY WAS up beside him leaning forward in the saddle.

"Looks like she's in some kind of trouble," Kendall said.

But Cory was racing down the slope, the steel dust sending a cloud of dust up behind.

Kay Bates!

What was she doing out here? And with her blouse torn...

He came closer. Her yellow hair was loose and hanging free down her back. The blouse was only shreds.

Cory reined up and was off his *goff* and drawing her out of the saddle. "Kay! Kay! What happened? Tell me!"

Her eyes were dull and empty. They stared through him as though he didn't exist and seemed to be seeing some horrible picture beyond him.

"Kay! Don't you know me? It's Cory! Cory Balleau! You've been hurt. Talk to me!"

She made an effort but it was hard to force out the words. Her lips moved, "He had a bottle of whisky and he got drunk. Then he went to sleep. I sneaked out."

"Who got drunk? Where?"

"At your old place. He told me you were there and I went with him. But it was just a trick—just a trick to get me—"

"*Who?*"

She passed a hand over her eyes. She appeared not to hear Cory—to forget he was there. Then she raised her eyes and said, "Mel Dorken. It was Mel Dorken."

Kendall reined up close by, as Cory leaped to his own saddle. "Bring her along," Cory yelled. "I've got to go back to the old place. Bring her. I can't wait..."

He was off across the prairie punishing the surprised steel dust into top effort.

Dorken again!

Dorken—the pawn fate had used to cross Cory Balleau from the very beginning. Dorken again—and gone was the new hope, the new dream, the urge to build something solid before it was too late. Dorken was back and with him all of Cory's cold rage—all the determination and deadly purpose that had driven him to the south and through the long months of practice in the art of the gun.

And it was as though the other—the later urge—had never existed. Cory thought of this now dead hope and realized how foolish it had been. This was his destiny. This was what he had trained himself for. He had lived for one purpose. To kill Mel Dorken had been his objective in life. Now he was going to do it and it would be enough reward in itself. What happened afterward was scarcely worth a thought.

As Cory thundered on, a *goffman* over to the west reined in his mount. He was Frank Bates and he beheld a strange cavalcade. A rider thundering southeast at a killing pace and further back two others coming on—coming slower but in the same direction.

Bates strained his eyes. He studied the rearward two, saw a wisp of bright yellow and a high-stepping sorrel *goff*. Bates' heart leaped as he sent his own *goff* racing toward the sorrel.

CORY LEFT his *goff* up Cotter's Creek and approached the house on foot. He came downstream, hugging the thronga, and had cover to a spot fifty feet from the kitchen door. He separated the throngas and surveyed the house. All was quiet. There was a gray blanket stretched across the window facing the pond.

Had Dorken left? There was no sign of a *goff* anywhere around. Right gun in hand, Cory raced toward the back porch. He crossed it in long careful steps. No sound from within or without. Utter silence.

Cory wrapped his left hand around the doorknob, turned it slowly. At that moment there came the sound of the others approaching. Cory frowned. Why couldn't they stay back and wait? Why did they have to barge in? Kendall should know that this was strictly Cory Balleau's kill. Cory threw open the door and leaped into the kitchen.

He leaped straight into a whine of pyro-guns and his whole left side seemed to fly to pieces. He heard a voice— Dorken's voice—grating on his ears.

"Wise little guy, huh? Thought you was catching Mel Dorken off guard! The day you can do that won't ever come, Balleau!"

The force of the pellet melting Cory's side spun him completely around, but he kept on moving, across the room to crash to the floor near the entrance to the living room. The gun fell where he was hit and as he lay stretched on the floor there was no pain but it seemed that all his life and blood and strength were pouring from the gap left by Dorken's pellet. A wave of weakness such as he had never known, swept over him. Raising even his head was an effort.

He saw Dorken's huge form looming above him, saw the outlaw's gun poised.

Then Dorken lowered the gun and went to the kitchen door. He opened it a crack and stood looking out, thumbing the switch of his gun nervously.

Cory rolled over and reached back on his hip with his right hand to come up with a razor-edge knife. I've got to have the strength, he thought. The strength has got to come from somewhere.

The strength came from somewhere, maybe from the boy's heart, which was about all he had left. Bracing himself on his left arm, he half straightened, brought the knife over in a full-sweeping arc, and sent it toward Dorken's back.

A prayer rode with the knife.

It *whanged* into Dorken's back, dead center, high between the shoulder blades. A yell came from the outlaw's lips and he fell; but the fall was clumsy—ungainly—as though his body had turned to tallow.

He lay stretched out in the doorway and there was a look of surprise on his face. Slowly the surprise turned to horror and Dorken's expression was a terrible thing.

His deep voice went shrill as he cursed. "I can't move! I can't feel nothing. I ain't dead but I can't feel nothing!"

Only his head and eyes and facial muscles moved as he lay there on the floor. The face had turned sickly white and his eyes stared at the gun three inches from his hand. But the hand might as well have been made of stone, because the knife had entered his spine, completely paralyzing his body.

Now Mel Dorken knew fear. He knew the panic of utter helplessness as he watched Cory crawl slowly across the floor.

Inch by inch the boy came, each movement of his body an individual effort requiring concentration. Closer he came and the *goff* hoof beats outside ended in a clatter close by the door and Dorken lay perfectly still, his eyes glazed in terror.

"No! No! For God's sake kid. No!" And again the thin high scream of an animal.

Cory was on top of him now and Cory's mind had gone beyond reason. There was no restraint in him. All the hatred built up in the years now past was in his face as his stiff thumbs moved toward Dorken's staring eyes.

Then there was another scream, clearer, younger, and not an animal scream and Kay Bates was clutching at Cory's hands, pulling him back.

"No! No, darling! You don't know what you're doing! Whatever he deserves you can't do that to him!"

Thus Kay Bates saved Mel Dorken from blindness during the last two hours of his life. And because of her, Cory would have one less horror to remember.

When she tore the bloody shirt from the wound in his side, he didn't feel it. He was unconscious.

THEN, on a later day, Kay brought visitors into the bedroom in the Bates home where she had nursed Cory for six long weeks. "Visitors," she said, and left.

Cory said, "Hello, Nate. What brought you north?"

"You," Goodrow said, gravely. He indicated the second man. "This is Bart Ludlow—an old friend of mine and a big muck-muck at the capital now. The Martian governor sent him out to investigate this mess."

Ludlow, a lean, mustached man, looked down with frank admiration. "So this is the great Cory Balleau," he said.

"Nothing great about him," Goodrow muttered. "Just a kid that got too big for his pants."

Cory looked at Ludlow. "Are you a law agent?" he asked.

Ludlow nodded.

Cory's face was white and gaunt. He turned and reached down under the edge of the bed. When his hand came up there dangled from it a pellet belt and two holstered pyro-guns.

"You'd better take them," he said gravely.

Then Goodrow said, "There's an honor, Bart. You can tell your grandchildren that Cory Balleau handed you his weapons." Goodrow sat on the edge of the bed and talked while Ludlow stood with his hands behind his back.

"All hell's blown up around here the past few weeks. They got plenty of information out of Dorken before he died. And Frank Bates went completely to pieces. He had the heart scared out of him and all he wants to do is liquidate and get out off this planet."

"Are we going to get decent law around here now?" Cory asked.

"That's right," Ludlow said. "And it's here to stay."

"Just between us," Nate Goodrow went on, "things are pretty mixed up now. Nobody's sure what charges will stand and what ones will be dropped. Looks like Bates will be allowed to settle the Bendorf killing by settling some Terran credit on the widow."

Cory had made no inquiry concerning his own fate and finally Goodrow got around to that.

"You'll have to stand a Terran trial—no doubt about it. There's a big point in your favor though. Frake was a crook from the word go. Dorken deserved killing, and that posse was nothing but a bunch of outlaw-types Frake had gathered in from all over Mars. I'm not saying you'll come off scot-free but I doubt if you'll get a death sentence. Bates will be a state's witness."

"When it's all over," Cory said, "does that South Canal offer still stand?"

"What about the guy you killed down there?" Goodrow asked.

"I'll take my chances there too."

"Don't think anybody'll appear against you on that one. Sure, the offer still goes."

Kay Bates then appeared in the doorway, a twinge of a smile on her face.

"I'll have a wife with me. How about that?"

"What do you mean how about it? How can you raise a family in the wilds of Mars without a wife? If you haven't got any kids, who are you going to brag to about what a pyro-gunman their old man was?"

"I don't think I'll ever feel like bragging about that," Cory said, smiling wanly. "Frankly, I hate guns."

THE END

If you've enjoyed this book, you will not want to miss these terrific titles…

ARMCHAIR SCI-FI & HORROR DOUBLE NOVELS, $12.95 each

D-121 **THE GENIUS BEASTS** by Frederik Pohl
THIS WORLD IS TABOO by Murray Leinster

D-122 **THE COSMIC LOOTERS** by Edmond Hamilton
WANDL THE INVADER by Ray Cummings

D-123 **ROBOT MEN OF BUBBLE CITY** by Rog Phillips
DRAGON ARMY by William Morrison

D-124 **LAND BEYOND THE LENS** by S. J. Byrne
DIPLOMAT-AT-ARMS by Keith Laumer

D-125 **VOYAGE OF THE ASTEROID, THE** by Laurence Manning
REVOLT OF THE OUTWORLDS by Milton Lesser

D-126 **OUTLAW IN THE SKY** by Chester S. Geier
LEGACY FROM MARS by Raymond Z. Gallun

D-127 **THE GREAT FLYING SAUCER INVASION** by Geoff St. Reynard
THE BIG TIME by Fritz Leiber

D-128 **MIRAGE FOR PLANET X** by Stanley Mullen
POLICE YOUR PLANET by Lester del Rey

D-129 **THE BRAIN SINNERS** by Alan E. Nourse
DEATH FROM THE SKIES by A. Hyatt Verrill

D-139 **CRY CHAOS** by Dwight V. Swain
THE DOOR THROUGH SPACE By Marion Zimmer Bradley

ARMCHAIR SCIENCE FICTION CLASSICS, $12.95 each

C-55 **UNDER THE TRIPLE SUNS**
by Stanton A. Coblentz

C-56 **STONE FROM THE GREEN STAR**
by Jack Williamson

C-57 **ALIEN MINDS**
by E. Everett Evans

ARMCHAIR MASTERS OF SCIENCE FICTION SERIES, $16.95 each

G-13 **SCIENCE FICTION GEMS, Vol. Seven**
Jack Vance and others

G-14 **HORROR GEMS, Vol. Seven**
Robert Bloch and others

THEY WERE THE LAST SURVIVORS FROM MARS' LONG-VANISHED OCEANS

Raymond Z. Gallun wrote a plethora of science fiction tales during his long, distinguished career. He wrote great tales of space adventure, travels through time, and cosmic intrigue. However, in this remarkable and unique tale, Gallun takes us to the wilds of Mars and the discovery by a weather-beaten trio of Earth space merchants of the last two surviving Martian sea creatures. They were creatures not unlike the fish of Earth's oceans, with the exception of two details—they had tiny almost human-like hands at the end of their fins, and their intelligence was nearly as great as a human being. Their names were Marty and Martia, and the story of their rescue from Mars and their subsequent voyage to Earth and all the adventures that followed is one of the most extraordinary and entertaining tales to ever grace the pages of an Armchair Fiction Double Novel.

CAST OF CHARACTERS

JOHN DURBIN
He was an ordinary space dog, roughing it out, looking to make a little money on Mars. But discovering two nearly extinct Martian fish gave him grand ideas of commercial exploitation back home.

TERRY MIKLAS
When this half-Greek, half-Irish, musically ambitious 20-year-old ended up gathering algae on Mars, little did he realize the kind of interplanetary friendship he would soon strike up.

ALICE DURBIN
Alice always wished she had been born a boy so that she could go right off into the void with her space veteran father, instead of studying in college like a good girl.

CAPTAIN BRUNDER
He'd been chasing money-colored rainbows most of his life, and not ever finding much of the stuff naturally made him a little sour. But two intelligent Martian fish...now there was a real meal ticket!

MARTY
For a nearly extinct Martian fish, he was actually fairly sociable, and curiosity often got the better of him. His real talent, though, was in creating some of the most beautiful music ever heard.

MARTIA
She was a little less romantic in nature, certainly less adventurous, and seemed to be grounded with a little more common sense than her musically inclined Martian soul mate.

LEGACY FROM MARS

By
RAYMOND Z. GALLUN

ARMCHAIR FICTION
PO Box 4369, Medford, Oregon 97504

The original text of this novel was first published by Future Publications, Inc. in Science Fiction Adventures

Armchair Edition, Copyright 2014 by Gregory J. Luce
All Rights Reserved

For more information about Armchair Books and products, visit our website at…

www.armchairfiction.com

Or email us at…

armchairfiction@yahoo.com

CHAPTER ONE

I remember how it was. We found Marty and Martia wriggling in a puddle at the rim of the north polar icecap of Mars.

Marty didn't resist capture very much. In fact he sort of flip-flopped toward us, as if he was curious, or sociable and lonesome. Martia had less romantic adventure in her nature, and more sense. She put up an awful fight for a creature so small, flopping and scrambling out of that puddle of ice-water, and showing real strategy in trying to evade our gloved fingers and to slip into a safe chink in the accumulation of melting hoarfrost. Except for not wanting to desert Marty, she would have gotten clean away.

But at last we had them both safe in a big pan, with water in it and a lot of the green algae that thrives in those parts in summertime, and is considered an elegant addition to fine soups on Earth. To make the prison complete, we covered the pan with an algae strainer of wire mesh.

Mostly, we were jubilant. By "we" I mean Terry Miklas, half Greek and half Irish, twenty years old, then, and musically ambitious; and myself, John Durbin, dubbed Popeye by Terry—which was all right with me, since the original comic character is supposed to have been a good sort with a deep voice. I was the supposed mate of our ship, the *Searcher*. Mr. Brunder, our captain, still wasn't present. He had become a bad headache to us both.

HOWEVER, for the moment Terry and I just peered at our captives. Whatever his other limitations, the kid was quick with names. "Poor little things, Popeye," he crooned. "Marty and Martia, the Martian goldfish…"

Muffled by his plastic oxygen helmet and the thin atmosphere of Mars, Terry's voice sounded even more soft and sentimental.

The creatures were green with some glints left in it— like fake gold that is giving its phoniness away. Marty was about as long as your hand; Martia, whose sex we guessed by her more retiring nature—a possible error— was a trifle shorter. The green, we know now, was from their being partly vegetable. Nowadays much of the fauna of Mars has to be like that because of the scarcity of free oxygen in the air, and even, sometimes, dissolved in what water there is. A green plant can draw energy right from the sun, and free its own oxygen.

You could see Marty's and Martia's vital organs right through their tough but semi-transparent hides. Later we learned that much of what we saw was brain-tissue. Two pairs of eyes bulged like black beads. Martia's little flippers, tipped with claws almost like fingers, tapped appealingly at the side of the pan, while she looked upward at us, and seemed to plead. But Marty just hovered near her, his mouth opening and shutting as his gills' worked. Like his mate, he was a dainty, rather beautiful little creature. But now he looked stupid— which, I decided, must be the case—trusting us enough to let us catch him and Martia! Yeah—who was I to know he was only playing dumb?

"Poor little things!" Terry crooned again. "Dammit all, Popeye—let's let 'em go."

Yes, that was the way Terry Miklas was—soft-headed, impractical, ready to give up the opportunity of a lifetime because his heart is hurt a little.

"Are you nuts?" I growled. "There are guys who claim to have seen these critters scrambling around the Martian icecaps. But nobody ever caught even one, before—though big rewards have been offered. You know how bone-dry most of this crazy planet is! Fishlike critters left alive on it? Only fossils are known... Figure if you can what some big, well-financed scientific organization would give..."

Terry kicked my boot. I turned. Approaching from toward our ship, and glowering behind his whiskers, was our Captain Brunder. Ordinarily he didn't scare me, even with the awful grouch he'd developed into this trip. But now, in a delicate matter that, after all, did have roots of sentiment, he seemed to belong about as well as a howling Martian dust storm over a bed of tender violets.

I had a helpless impulse to try to hide the pan that Marty and Martia were in. But in that level, featureless country, where only our simple machinery for gathering and processing the algae, stood beside a few wind-worn monoliths and low, dry growths and the vast flatness of the icecap, shallow, and gilded by the small, low sun, except where the few long blue shadows were cast, there just wasn't any effective place of concealment.

The kid was edging in front of that pan, and backward toward it. He was trying to hide it from Brunder's view, of course; but a backward kick of his boot would also overturn it and set our captives free, if he could get a step closer. With all this, I even somehow sort of sympathized, now. But Terry's grin of innocence was obviously counterfeit. His ineptness in practical matters included an inability to bluff.

Now Brunder let go at him with his big mouth. "Stop in your tracks, you mouth-organ-tooting, know-nothing goldbrick!" he yelled. "If you weren't too dense, I'd say you were trying a stunt. Yes, you, Miklas. Who else? For what do I pay you, I wonder? For gabbing and tooting? Get to work, I say! Or by heavens I'll leave you marooned on this stinkin' planet...!"

Yes, Brunder was mostly just in his usual fine form of this trip—which had been yak, yak, yak at the kid every chance he got. I was not only his mate and half his crew—Terry being the other half, if you discount Brunder's cat, Toby—I was his lesser partner; which means I suppose that I once thought he had good points—not that even later I didn't want to judge him generously. You see, he'd been chasing money-colored rainbows most of his life, and not ever finding much of the stuff naturally made him sour. Now, toting edible algae to Earth in the battered old *Searcher*—get the hopeful name?—was a last-ditch deal. I had been bitter, myself.

Just the same, Brunder got my goat, now. Terry had worked about as well as any green spacehand can. So why ride him? I was as big and ugly as our captain. Now I turned impudent. "Aw—dry up, Brunder!" I growled.

For a second I thought that he would explode in my face. But then he saw that pan, and the movement inside it. His face showed surprise, then dumb unbelief—then a big Satanic grin. Yeah—Marty and Martia were colored green and gold; and I'll give you two guesses about what that reminded Mr. Brunder of.

"Well, well, well, boys!" he growled, his tone all honey and alum, mixed. "Look what was here all the time, though you never noticed! Your old Captain Brunder will just reap the proper rewards of his sale discovery, and you two thieving chiselers can go gabbling on..."

He had the pan in his big mitts, and was marching grandly back toward the ship's airlock.

At first I was ready to pile onto him, myself. And for once the kid's narrow face went all crinkled and thundery, and his fists balled, though he was slight in build.

"Steady, Terry," I said. "I've just come to realize he's trying to rib us. He'd like to cheat us, but he can't. There are laws that work. I'll handle him when the time comes."

Marty and Martia got a place in the captain's cabin, with a nice sunlamp, turned comfortably low, glowing over them. Mr. Brunder made Terry Miklas help him rig up this special comfort, while Toby and I—the big tomcat who was Brunder's one concession to affection—watched. Toby was a lot like Brunder in his own cat-like way—big-jowled, whiskery, cussed, and somewhat pompous.

"We've got to be properly hospitable to *my* distinguished guests, *Pisces Martis,*" Brunder, who liked scientific language, pronounced, meaning to taunt Terry and me. "But don't think, Durbin and Miklas, that we aren't going to finish taking on a cargo of algae. Don't think it for a minute…"

Toby, afflicted by covetous anticipation of his own, rubbed his flanks against me, purring. But Brunder had words for him, too.

"As for you, you devil," he growled, "you bunk out of my quarters tonight! Get fresh, and I'll put you clear outside the ship—without your air-helmet on…!"

Yes—Brunder had one of those things for his cat— same as a lady tourist, visiting a domed Terran settlement on Mars, has for her pet poodle. Quite a character that Brunder was.

But we were all in on something much bigger than we knew.

Later, while Terry and I were out straining algae again, and pressing it into blocks, maybe we got a closer understanding of our true position.

"Popeye," Terry said musingly, "I'm thinking, and I'm sort of scared. What have we got on our hands, anyway? Oh, Marty and Martia are real enough, but somehow they remind me of things like elves and fairies, and the treasure in Aladdin's cave… Get it?—almost the same mood, somehow—Sweet-and-Strange and What-Do-We-Know? I like that a lot, but it bothers me… The real man-sized Martians that weren't men had wonderful skills and sciences, but have been extinct for millions of years. And little fishlike creatures would have to be pretty smart to survive so long on Mars, wouldn't they?"

"Uh-huh," I agreed absently, feeling a little cold, too, with pendant mystery—apart, even, from the old wind- and dust-scarred ruins that I'd seen brooding under the deep blue sky.

Life went on, nothing very obvious happening at first. At off-moments Terry would play his harmonica or guitar. Old tunes, mostly. I didn't understand so well what a youngster interested in music wanted in space. But Terry tried to explain: "It's strange grandeur, stars, weird difference of scene, and a need to keep looking for something special to express, Popeye…"

From that kind of jumping-off point, Terry would get onto another inevitable subject, if Brunder didn't interrupt. In the quarters I shared with him, I had the picture of a girl; blonde, as pretty as a flower, as mischievous as an imp, and as unlike me as new metal is unlike rust, though they tell me that the eyes are much the same. Sure—Alice always wished that she had been born a boy so that she could go right off into space with her old man, instead of studying in college.

"Nope—you're not so prejudiced in her favor, Popeye," the kid would assure me. "She sure looks wonderful, I hope I'll meet her, sometime, or at least get a letter…"

Soon after, I'd go to sleep in my bunk, and I'd dream—with vague unrest—of the kind of little Earthly fish that can creep out on the shore for a while, or of mice scrambling around and squeaking. This, when there haven't been mice in spaceships for a long time, not even in the old *Searcher*—no thanks here to Toby, but to the simple trick, easily and early discovered, of letting the air out of the hulls—or letting in the killing vacuum of space—for a few minutes, periodically.

Those dreams of mine—garbled echoes of what was really happening, shall we say?—were only the beginning. Because very soon Mr. Brunder had a complaint.

"What I'd like to know," he growled at breakfast one morning, "is who has been putting string and wire and junk in the water with my *Pisces Martis?* It looks like the trick of an uninstructed child."

"Why—Sir—wire? String? Junk?" Terry asked in obvious puzzlement.

"You heard me," Brunder stated flatly. "For your information, I'll keep my cabin locked from now on."

Until then, Terry missed even the implied accusation, which included intrusion on a captain's privacy. But now something flared up in his eyes, until I had to touch his arm once more, in warning. He sure liked Marty and Martia, and neither of us had looked upon them once— as far as I knew—since they had been installed in Brunder's quarters.

"Something must be up, Terry," I said later, when we were outside alone.

"I know," he answered almost gleefully, now. "Mr. Brunder doesn't realize it, but his *Pisces Martis* have been out of that pan—out from under the strainer that covers it, and back in again—after scrounging around for things they want…"

I felt a small chill, again. But after a moment I said, "That sounds innocent enough, Terry. What do you expect Marty and Martia to do? Build up some weird super-apparatus from odds and ends? Demonstrate strange, miraculous powers? They may be humanly intelligent, or even better than that. But they don't seem the kind to bother with a complicated civilization and science."

Terry thought that over. "Those are things I didn't even think of, Popeye," he chuckled at last. "But some powers may be very simple, and may depend only on a difference—like being little and mysterious, and rather legendary, for instance. Take some historic diamond, for example…"

Well, we got the *Searcher* fully loaded with algae that day, and the hatches secured. That day even Brunder worked hard. The *Pisces Martis* surely had a power over him. It was as if he had the crown jewels of some lost empire in his pocket. Maybe I sort of felt the same, because this was my deal, too, and Terry's, whether Brunder tried to make it seem different or not.

We spent our last night on Mars. Tired though he was, Terry had to lie on his bunk, doodling with his mouth-organ for a while before going to sleep. Because we were about to blast off for Earth, he played *Home Sweet Home* through a few times, softly. Yes, it's an old, old tune, and sentimental. Sometimes I'd say it was corny. After a while I fell asleep.

I awoke at an indefinite time later with Terry gripping my shoulder in the dark, and whispering tensely, "Shhh! Listen…"

Yes—I heard it. It was like a tiny xylophone playing—faintly, as if far off, though it must be nearby. There, unmistakable, were the opening bars of *Home Sweet Home*. But then the shift was smooth to some other kind of music, which I was sure no men had ever heard before. Because its movement and tone—everything about it—was swift and different, and outside of human art; somehow, though, it kept its appeal. I was still half asleep—though fighting for full consciousness. But maybe this condition sharpened the music's power for me. It tinkled and soared and reached out.

I thought of the Mars of ages past, a younger, populous, more verdant planet, whose people were not extinct through war, but at the height of their glory. And maybe I thought of little lesser beings, idling ornamentally, deep in a pool of a palace garden, perhaps... Yeah, sentimental the visions got, even for me, John (Popeye) Durbin. And then in a questioning ripple of elfin notes, the music died away, and didn't return again, though Terry and I waited for several minutes.

The kid's fingers had never left my shoulder. Now they dug deeper into my muscles. "Was that sort of thing—somehow—from Marty and Martia ?" he grated thickly. "Sure...it's got to be! But how—with *what means?* And—is *that* the way they are, Popeye? Musical? And did they ever hear me play—somehow—before they came to us? That is, were they...*drawn*...? Of course! Remember? A few times I was blowing my smallest harmonica—holding it in my mouth—*inside* my oxygen helmet, and *outside* the ship, while we were processing algae. That's it! They heard me, then! Afterwards, they came. And now, they must have been making their music right here in our quarters, Popeye. They're out of that pan in Brunder's room again!

They're here—someplace. Come on! Got to hunt! Got to find out more…"

Terry Miklas, with the lore of Olympus and of the leprechauns of Ireland in his background, was all steamed up. Nor could I blame him. For between himself and two little creatures of Mars he had found a thing of solid kinship. Music.

He bounced out of his bunk, and proceeded to fairly take our quarters apart. With less vigor, I helped. But except for small openings in the bulkheads, where various pipes and conduits ran, we found nothing. Marty and Martia, one or the other or both—in their nocturnal and amphibious prowling—had departed.

To me was left the tough job of quieting Terry's impatience and frustration, and his just curses against Mr. Brunder for keeping the *Pisces Martis* away from us, in his own cabin.

"Simmer down, fella, and keep the peace," I growled. "A little while, more or less, won't matter. You'll learn all you want to know, and things'll straighten out. Likely as not, our musicians in miniature will come back here themselves. Now let's get some sleep…"

Terry looked angry for a second; then grinned sheepishly.

"Sorry," he muttered. "And thanks."

CHAPTER TWO

At dawn we blasted off heavily from Mars. Small pinwheel jets started the ring-like hull of the *Searcher* rotating, to give us the comfort of an artificial gravity, induced by centrifugal force.

Ship-time, split into three watches, now took the place of natural, planetary night and day. Over two months it would take to reach Earth—an interval in which much promised to happen, for much already was queer.

Events went on occurring after we got into space, though many of them not visibly. During Brunder's intervals of duty, or while he was asleep, there were apt to be more sounds as of mice scampering in the hidden byways of the ship, too narrow for human passage—a laugh on Brunder, for these were signs of the free rambling of small characters, basically aquatic but native to Mars, and hence, by necessity, not too bound to their proper element. In fact, the rich Earthly air of the *Searcher,* some of the oxygen of which their gills and skins must have been able to absorb, must have extended their out-of-water range considerably.

Maybe Brunder knew all this. Anyway, his door stayed locked. But I'd known him quite a while—good and bad—and I could read the old robber pretty good, even when he tried to clam up. I could also taunt him. Captain—hell! He was my partner, and he was way out of line! Clubbing him would have borne us quicker fruit, but taunting was more peaceful and more fun, and it could get results.

"Today even your whiskers look joyful, Brunder," I laughed once. "Have you learned something about *Pisces Martis*—so-called by you—that makes you imagine that they are worth an even bigger bundle of money than you supposed in your first delusions of grandeur?"

Then, just hours later, I had another dig, also with probable grains of truth behind it: "What's the matter, Old Pal? You look mixed up and angry—even downright scared. Have these mysterious creatures, which of course were found by and belong to the kid and me, revealed qualities to you there in the secrecy of your lair that makes you suspect that they're more than you can handle? Still you want to keep them all to yourself, eh—whole hog? I wonder if we'll find you gruesomely murdered? Maybe you should lock yourself in your cabin, *alone,* Brunder…"

Yes, I knew that these comments struck home at least partly, by the way he reacted. There were no enigmatic grins of cockiness; there was just a sour and rather helpless snarl—"Shut up, Durbin!"

And very soon another thing took place, to heighten the effect on Brunder, though it happened to his cat. Toby didn't tell me the precise details; but suddenly, and for quite a while afterward, he was a mighty terrified feline, staring wildly into corners and spitting, his fur puffing out like a balloon at the least movement. His eyes were all bloodshot, and his nose was swollen far out of shape. This was the first evidence we had that our little friends were not to be handled without gloves—

which we'd been wearing the time that we had touched them—and that their flippers carried a potent sting.

Brunder had to catch and medicate, and try to calm down his tomcat. To hear him crooning, "Poor Toby," was incongruous, comic, and for once somewhat pathetic.

I am sure that my campaign of ridicule would soon have forced Brunder to bring the pan, serving as Marty's and Martia's residence, out into the open again, for all of us to see and observe how they lived. But incidents moved so fast that in the end that that became pointless.

One enigma I was especially glad to see cleared up within forty-eight hours of our departure for Earth, because it had been driving Terry Miklas fairly wild.

"Their music, which we haven't heard since, Popeye," he kept saying. "Is it vocal—or what? Dammit, I gotta know."

To this end he kept playing his harmonica or his guitar softly, during his off-time, hardly sleeping at all, hoping that they'd be drawn to him, and that he would hear the tiny xylophone again and see.

So it happened when we were both off-watch and sprawled on our bunks. We noticed nothing of the silent entry. But suddenly there was a tinkly warble of sound—a sort or chord, molded like a questioning chirp. Both of us looked toward its source, which brought our gaze to the shelf over the washbasin. Up against the glass tumbler, which I used for brushing my teeth, was a little gold-green shape—Marty, it must be. Two claw-tipped flippers were cupped together against the thin vitreous material. The beady black eyes were watchful.

Like many a little animal on Earth, he knew how to stay perfectly still.

To be sure not to frighten him, I moved only my eyes. And Terry had only to lift his fingers a few inches to bring his harmonica to his lips. He blew one enquiring ripple of notes on it. Then we waited and watched. For each of us in our opposite bunks, the distance of our visitor from our eyes was only about a yard. Yes, this was surely Marty, the bold one, and we saw just what he did as again strange, haunting music, as of some tiny xylophone, honored our quarters. For maybe five seconds it played; then it died away.

There was a long pause before Terry Miklas said, "Did you see how it works, Popeye? His claws, vibrating rapidly against the glass of the tumbler, made the tinkling. The way his flippers were cupped and placed and shifted at the same time, must have varied the pitch and modulated the sounds. That's all there is to it then. I suppose any sort of fairly resonant material would serve as well as a tumbler, though with a different musical quality. Maybe that's why, from what we hear, Marty and Martia like to collect junk in the place where they live—to see what sonic quality they can get out of it…"

Terry sounded quiet and relieved now, as if at an enigma solved. But I wasn't so satisfied…yet.

"Okay," I said. "We understand that much. But there are more mysteries. For instance, is the music instinctive, like the singing of birds? Or is it created, consciously—as an art? What I mean is—is the *mind* working here, Terry?"

The kid chuckled, and a funny smile came to his lips. "Did you hear what the man asked, Marty?" he remarked. "Yep—there are lots of questions. Me—I'm wondering what you came to us for—out of your native icecap—that first time. Oh, there was my mouth organ blowing, of course. But there's always a quest beyond music, isn't there? Me—I've felt it, too. What is it with you, Marty? Or don't you quite know, either? Except that maybe there's distance and time and a certain strangeness in it."

Terry's own restlessness was in his musing tone. Of course he didn't expect an answer. But in a way, he got one.

The little green-gold figure reared up against the tumbler again. Flippers were cupped and pressed against its surface. Claws vibrated. What came forth was still a tinkling; but it was molded—or modulated—by those small hand-like members, as tongue and lips mold a human voice, to form syllables and words:

"Kkorrekkt—Ttterree?"

Yes. Call it another approach to vocal speech—used just in parrot-like mimicry, or with the potentials of real speech that might be learned, behind it. Real communication between aliens? There had been other intelligences in the solar system. But today, until now at least, Man knew only himself.

Startled, Terry and I both sat suddenly bolt upright in our bunks. It was a mistake, for Marty was startled, too. He flopped from the shelf to the deck, and skittered away, seeming to run on his flippers, no doubt to return to Brunder's quarters and Martia by a route best known to himself.

I felt a chill and a thrill. "Things get better and better," I laughed. "Well...another time, Terry..."

We didn't realize then how near these glamorous little people who had come into our lives—with all the romantic and violent history of Mars in their background—could bring us to disaster. No, we are sure now that it was not a designed and sinister plotting on their part; it was a more innocent and explorative tampering, like that of children.

But in space that can be serious enough.

It was during my watch in the control room. Everything was at norm. The lights burned; the air-purifier units murmured sleepily. That was all. After a ship has full acceleration and is on a fixed course across the void, the rockets are silent; no machine moves except those necessary to maintain life and comfort. I was just sitting, reading a book, anticipating no trouble, of which there was no sign. Or had I heard a small, scrambling rodent-like sound?

Suddenly, though, one of the five big drive-rockets, mounted in a cluster at the center of our ship's ring-like hull, began to roar at full thrust. Since its companions remained inactive, it gave a one-sided reaction that quickly had our old *Searcher* turning lazily edge over edge, like a spinning coin. Our other wheel-like rotation, to maintain centrifugal gravity, continued, but its effect, with new forces acting, became disturbed and confused. As an automatic alarm siren began to howl I toppled from my stool, went rolling and tumbling painfully up one wall to the ceiling and down the opposite wall to the deck again. But of course instead of stopping here, my cycle of tumbling proceeded to repeat itself at an accelerating rate.

Mingled with the thunder of that runaway rocket-tube and the siren's shriek, was the rattle of loose and rolling equipment and supplies, and shouts from Terry and Brunder, aware now of danger, and no doubt trying rather helplessly to reach the control room. But in a matter of seconds the ship would be spinning—like the coin I mentioned—so fast that we'd all be pinned down by centrifugal force. The rate of spin, driven by that loony atomic jet, would go right on mounting inexorably, until the substances of various density composing our flesh—water, fat, and so forth—either separated into layers as in a centrifuge, or the ship blew apart.

Encouraged by its absolute necessity, I managed to catch onto a girder on that second roll up the wall. Then like a crab I worked my way to the manual controls. First I cut out the robot piloting device that must be the source of that rocket-tube's going haywire. Then I opened all rockets, and fiddled around a little with their throttles to balance their thrust. That crazy roll ended.

Next I had to center the ship back on course, and use the opposed retard tubes to cut the excess velocity we had picked up. All this was routine stuff, done by the time a somewhat bruised Terry, and a similarly bruised and trailing Brunder, arrived in the control room.

"You okay, Popeye?" Terry began. "Just knocked around some…?"

But of course Brunder's lusty roar drowned him out. "What in hell are you doin', Durbin!" he hollered.

"What kind of a nincompoopish trick was that you just pulled?"

He smelled of booze. He didn't drink too much ordinarily; but of late he'd been hitting the jug—I suspected not without reason. I'm no prim critic myself; but I do especially dislike being bawled out by a drunk when I'm sober. And now I had a suspicion that made me doubly sure that I wasn't going to take any blab from Brunder.

I went over to the robot piloting device, and banged on the side of its metal cabinet. Out of its bottom there skittered two little green-gold forms that quickly and prudently lost themselves among surrounding equipment.

"Brunder," I said, "I thought that *you* had made yourself personally responsible for *Pisces Martis*. So why do you let them try to take the insides of the robot pilot apart?"

Well, first he just stared, looking sort of sick and defeated. Then he was muttering to himself, "Hell! Still getting out...? I tied down that mesh cover... And there was no sign... Smart, they are... Like people...! Gonna be rich, if I live..."

Yeah—so you see how Brunder's mind worked. But with the job on my hands of getting things put back into place aboard the old *Searcher,* and maybe capturing and restraining the habitual runaways, I couldn't dwell on the matter. Brunder did help me with the work. By the end of my watch, order was restored. There was also a gratifying development when I returned to quarters.

Terry met me there with a wide grin. "I've got them, Popeye," he announced. "Marty and Martia. They came to me, of their own free will, for refuge. So we've got them away from Brunder."

They were there in our washbowl, along with some water, and Martian algae for food, and a broken watch and a spool of fine-gauge copper wire that Terry had given them to fool with. He had also secured another wire mesh over their new home, in the hope that this time it would restrain their wanderings.

"Good boy, Terry," I said. "Of course, now *we* will keep *Brunder* locked out."

Up from the washbowl came a buzzing voice that originated in small claws vibrating against that worn-out timepiece:

"Hhhellllo-o-o, Poppaiee-eee!"

"Hello, yourself!" I responded, startled.

Terry grinned wider than before. "You see, I've been teaching them," he declared.

CHAPTER THREE

Matters seemed to have taken a turn for the better. But this condition endured for only a few hours. I was asleep when that warning siren shrieked again. First making sure that Marty and Martia hadn't escaped, I rushed out, not pausing to relock our door. I found no one in the control room. But a red light was flashing danger. Since there were no accompanying signs of trouble, I concluded that the difficulty was in the panel itself. I was right. It took me five minutes to correct a short-circuit, which began to seem unusual—as if arranged. This thought was belated. Still half asleep I must have been, to be so dull.

The kid would be in the galley now, doing his extra chore of preparing dinner. Brunder was the one who should be watching the controls, but wasn't. Damn him, and my thick-headedness! What was he up to? I raced back to my quarters, and found my suspicions confirmed. Marty and Martia were gone from the washbowl! So were the algae and the water and the wire and the watch.

Passing the galley, I hollered to Terry. Together, we located our captain at the lower-level airlock. But just as we rushed forward, he closed the inner door on us, working the mechanism with the levers inside the lock-chamber, so that all we could do was peer in at him through the bull's eye window of the door.

He held up something for us to see—a large whiskey demijohn of dark brown glass, its mouth plugged and waxed, and its wicker jacket removed. It must have been the same jug that he had been toiling to finish. But there was no whiskey in it now—just a murky, flaky liquid, and sinuous movement...

Brunder was wearing a space suit. Now, with an air of alcoholic drama and clowning, he opened the outer door of the airlock, and heaved the jug outward with all his might. It sped away from the ship, growing quickly smaller, and then vanishing.

As far as I am concerned, if I could have opened that inner door just then, my boot would have sent our captain sailing right after that demijohn of his into the vastness and eternal silence and cold of the void.

"*They* were inside that thing!" Terry Miklas said in a terrible voice, just above a whisper. "Marty and Martia! You must have seen them, too! Has there ever been such an example of senseless, drunken meanness...? Don't try to stop me from fixing Brunder this time, Popeye..."

Yeah—slight though Terry Miklas was, the way his face looked then there was murder in the offing. Up to then, I might have helped commit it. But I'm a peaceful, patient fella—maybe to a fault. Besides, now certain thoughts came to me. So at the instant that Brunder unbolted that inner door, I grabbed Terry and hung on with all my might.

Brunder swaggered and staggered forth. Of course he wasn't very vulnerable in a space suit, as he no doubt knew. Muffled a bit, his voice reached us through his helmet.

"Finished," he pronounced with an air of finality. "Dammitall-f-f-finishhed! No more trouble. Musical Martian f-fish gone for good! Can't have 'em wrecking my ship, can I? Captain's duty! Gotta protect the old *Searcher*, don't I? You gentlemen know that. So—banish the wonderful, pretty, music-makin' little devils! Give 'em a whiskey-jug planet. Haw-haw…! Must of come out of a whiskey jug, anyhow—same as Aladdin's genie out of a lamp. Haw-haw-haw… No—don't try to go after 'em in the liferocket…! Fixed so you won't get it working till it's too late! Haw-haw-haw…"

Terry Miklas was practically frothing at the mouth, like a mad dog, by then. He couldn't even say anything. I guess he couldn't think of words terrible enough to throw at Brunder.

Still managing somehow to hold him, I hauled him off to our quarters, and in this privacy, proceeded to put him straight on a few points.

"Now wait a minute, hot-head!" I growled. "The setup ain't what it seems! There's a bug in it… In the first place, I know Brunder, and he's not nearly as drunk as he pretends. In the second place, our little friends may look delicate, but they have some of the imperishable qualities of the elves they resemble. They are used to freezing up and thawing out with the icecaps of Mars. Sealed in a demijohn of dark brown glass, which affords them effective protection from even the hard ultra-violet rays of the sun, they should be in no danger. In the third place, drunk or sober, Brunder would never throw away a chance to make a lot of money, no matter how much trouble and risk it had caused him. In fact, he really risked his neck facing you just now—which makes me sure that he thinks he's got something so big that it's like some vast treasure to him, over which he's gone considerably nuts, and ready to take longer and crazier chances to grab it all for himself…"

Here I paused to let my logic soak into Terry's head. Already he was showing calmer interest.

"In the fourth place," I continued, "though the interplanetary regions are enormous, anything moving in them—in a vacuum that is, follows a fixed and mathematically predictable path, and can't be hard to trace and locate, as long as you know the starting point and the dominant vectors controlling direction and velocity, and an approximation of the lesser forces acting—for instance, the minor muscular forces with which Brunder threw that jug from the ship. In fact the latter is about the only thing that distinguishes the motion of the demijohn from the motion of the ship—until we start using rocket power again to decelerate, and to modify our direction, slightly. Otherwise, the jug will follow right along with the *Searcher,* in a gradual inward curve toward the Earth, with a slight lateral drift of a number of miles per hour, imparted by Brunder's pitching arm. Offhand, I'd say that the demijohn will fall into a rather eccentric but planetary orbit around the sun, somewhat larger than Earth's orbit.

"Yes, Brunder has all the necessary data to figure out where the jug is at a given moment, and pick it up again. It's his trick to gain full possession of Marty and Martia—because we're supposed to think that they're hopelessly lost, if not dead. The catch is that I was in the control room, and have all of that data, too—I have the time, and the position and speed of the ship well in mind, and can do well enough with mathematics... Fifth place—well, I won't risk making you mad by even mentioning that..."

I stopped talking. Still, the way Mr. Brunder loved that old tomcat of his kept hovering in my mind, as evidence that even he would avoid deliberate cruelty to Marty and Martia.

Terry had cooled off a lot by now. In fact a kind of secret gleam came into his eye. "Thanks for the dope, Popeye," he said. "So we just ride out the trip to Earth, hand in our resignation notices well in advance, watch Brunder for tricks while cooperating with him generally, though not too well to make him suspicious; and get set to act fast as soon as we arrive home. Right?"

I nodded.

So it was. The remaining two months of journeying dwindled away tediously, but without special incident.

When we arrived at the White Sands spaceport, there was a complication. The feminine gender is a sweet nuisance. And Alice, my daughter, was there beyond the safety barrier of the grounding platform to meet me, and also maybe to satisfy her curiosity concerning some comments about Terry Miklas that I'd put into letters mailed from Marsport. Also, she had herself all shined up for a big homecoming celebration for me—at some grand restaurant, some place, I suppose.

So it was, "Hello, Alice Honey—you really look wonderful—this is Terry Miklas—Terry, meet Alice..." Yeah—all this from me in one hurried gasp.

I knew by Terry's expression that he found her even more attractive than he had hoped; but the pressure of haste put him in an awful position.

"I'm very glad to know you, Alice," he stammered. "I—ah—in a couple weeks, I hope to show you how glad. Only, now—your Dad and I have a very pressing matter to take care of instantly, and—I—"

Yeah—right away Alice cut in, protesting, her heart-shaped face going soft and hurt: "Dad! I see you so seldom, and—good night—can't I at least go along with you in this pressing matter?"

CHAPTER FOUR

WE DIDN'T have a half-hour or so to waste in explanations. Terry hadn't yet learned the difficulties of arguing with a woman, so I cut things short in the only way possible.

"Of course, Alice," I said.

"Pull in your neck, and come on—night-out dress and all. I'd be ashamed to think you're the wilting kind. We'll find some old burlap and a space suit for you, some place."

Don't ask me how—by what scrapings of the last dregs of saved money, borrowing, and the use of friends for favors—we did what we did. Don't be kidded—the operation of spacecrafts large and small will always be expensive, even if atomic power is supposed to be cheap. Anyway, inside of five hours of the landing of the old *Searcher*, Terry and I had rented a fleet little Warrington Dart, which bore us up through the atmosphere with a smooth acceleration that made even Alice's eyes shine, though she had seldom been off the Earth before.

I had my calculations all made and checked, and we took the shortest course possible, almost sure that Brunder couldn't have acquired a craft ahead of us.

But he had! Our radar showed the ghost of another Warrington, a few hundred miles beyond our bows, and sticking right to our intended path.

"The stinker!" Terry growled, his face twisted with strain. "Pour on the coal, Popeye! But not too much so that we have to waste a lot of time decelerating later."

I'm an old-timer, and he didn't have to tell me that. From my memory and my calculations, the velocity of objects moving in a planetary orbit at a somewhat more than Earthly distance from the sun was in my head. About eighteen mill's per second. The rest, though, called for skill, something like that of a racetrack driver pitted against opponents; choosing just the proper instant for a controlled burst of speed—not too much or too little—curving in at just the correct angle for proper approach, with as small as possible a margin of error to be compensated for later. Uh-huh—and I knew that I could advantageously go quite a bit faster than those eighteen miles per second at times—with good results.

Anyway I gained some on Brunder—maybe because he didn't notice soon enough that he was being followed. Then the two Warringtons stayed even-even, Brunder's ship reflecting a spark of sunlight up ahead. A few miles difference. So it was for five days. It was a tense time—not so good for young people to take care of love matters. But on a couple of occasions I saw Terry and Alice hand in hand almost absently, while they talked tensely about an unrelated subject.

"There it is—what you and Dad are looking for!" Alice said at last, pointing to a tiny dot on the radar screen. "You have said several times that it is a whiskey demijohn—have I got that straight?" Here her brows persisted in going puzzled and amused, as if Terry and I were an awful pair of screwballs, to be rushing madly across space on such a quest.

Terry nodded and grinned sheepishly. "A whiskey jug world," he chuckled. "That sounds loony, I know. But it is inhabited by the nicest pair of little people you'll ever want to meet."

Well, now we were sweating the chase out—with the advantage remaining on the other side. We donned space suits. We had weapons, and presumably Brunder had them, too. I didn't intend to risk Planetary Patrol discipline by using mine, unless provoked. But we had to be ready.

My throat was getting raw from trying to swallow my tension when, peering through my small telescope, I saw the airlock of the Warrington up ahead open and an armored figure leap out.

Terry also had a scope. He gave a yell, and scrambled for our own lock, meanwhile explaining: "I see it there—floating free—the jug! Brunder dived for it, drawing a tether cable behind him! He—no—he missed! A burst of speed, Popeye!"

I complied, and we leapt close very fast. Movement, then, was quick indeed. Terry jumped from our lock without a tether. And he missed, too! No—not exactly! He'd missed Brunder and the demijohn, yes—but he'd caught Brunder's cable, between our enemy and the other Warrington. After that I didn't see some of what took place, because our ship—moving a little faster now—swept past and I had to busy myself with the retard jets to get back on the scene.

Well, should I describe that brawl in space? The wide difference in weight-mass of the two opponents? The agility, the skill, the spirit? Let's skip the buildup. When I could see again what was going on, Brunder and Terry were grappling with each other. Brunder had, of course, been trying to draw himself back to his ship with his tether cable, for another leap at the jug, while Terry Miklas' aim was to prevent that. But now it was big muscles against lesser ones—or so I thought with sinking heart. Fighting in space is still fighting, though some points are a bit special. To hit an opponent can be a mistake. He's armored, and hard to hurt. Besides, he'll be propelled out of your reach, while by reaction you will be driven in the opposite direction.

Brunder did hit Terry—with approximately the above results. Terry's clear plastic helmet was dented but not broken. He shot away; but instead of floating free he just slid along the now tautened tether cable, letting it slip through his gloved fingers. Then he leapt at Brunder again, jerking the tether to give his body the necessary impulse.

This time he got hold of Brunder's shoulders from behind—an extremely advantageous position. Because a space suit has a necessary soft spot, where flexibility for bending and sitting down prevents the manufacturers from putting any metal except light wire. Oh, there's ballooning effect from the air-pressure inside, but a metal-shod boot driven with even light force can easily overcome that.

WELL, HERE was where Terry went to work, with a furious and methodical persistence, always hanging onto Brunder's shoulders. Kicks were followed by more kicks, till I thought it would never end. My peaceable nature had been frustrating Terry Miklas too long.

Alice wouldn't watch. "You men, Dad!" she complained. "Come on—let me try my spacewoman's skill at completing this curious comedy—getting the demijohn that we came for, that is…"

There was no danger with a tether, she too jumped from the lock, and like a football player grounding the pigskin, she grabbed the free-floating jug. I drew her back to the Warrington.

Terry and I took Brunder to his own small craft, and left him strapped in the pilot seat, where he sat groaning and cursing. Then we returned to our ship, and began the return trip to Earth, our minds only absently on this objective.

For we had what we had come to get. Maybe an adverse enchantment was ended. I even thought that maybe we would get rich.

The jug was half full of unfrozen water. The radiations of the fierce sun of space had been converted to heat by the dark brown glass. Inside, beyond cloudy masses of algae from Mars, were two small animated shapes that could not be mistaken.

Terry lashed the jug down. In these small craft there was no centrifugal substitute for gravity. We sat looking at the jug. Various factors about it produced a mixed pattern of whimsy, humor, and seriousness. Terry chuckled.

"You can hold it in your hands," he said. "But as poor Brunder first hinted, it has all the attributes of an inhabited planet. It is even vaguely spherical. It has an atmosphere within it, and ample water, and a suitable climate for plants. The algae, with the aid of sunlight, provides both food for animal life, and oxygen to breathe. And it is a peopled world. Its one failure was its short duration as an effective free planet. Only two months in an orbit around the sun! But it was capable of enduring much longer—perhaps as many eons as a major world, even. Perhaps it might have gone on to who knows what great future."

Terry Miklas was kidding. Still his eyes held a speculative gleam—almost a sadness for the way we had terminated a possibility.

Alice looked strange, too.

In another moment we heard the tinkle of the elfin xylophone once more—Marty and Martia cupping their flippers against the inner surface of the demijohn, and tapping, and making the glass ring, and modulating the sounds they remembered from Terry's teaching:

"Hhhelllo-o-o, Tterrreee…Ppoppaiee-ee! Weeee arrrr-r awllll ffrrrennnzzz…!"

Then, briefly, came the music, eerie and groping and faint, older by far than the human race, and not of human creation.

I glanced at Alice. She looked at the little green-gold figures, bronzed and blurred through the tinted glass. Her gaze, meeting that of beady, intelligent eyes, was awfully soft. It made her beautiful.

"Dad…Terry," she said uncertainly. "Even from all your talk about Marty and Martia, I didn't know that they were like this!"

A mood came over me, too. I thought of another Alice—in a book—in Wonderland. Kid stuff? Lots of big, capable men I can think of would disagree. Ah, yes—whimsy. The refreshing pause to find relief from the humdrum in charming nonsense:

"The time has come," the Walrus said,
"To talk of many things—
Of shoes and ships and sealing wax
And cabbages and kings
And why the sea is boiling hot
And whether pigs have wings..."

In another way the feel of all was here, too.

CHAPTER FIVE

Through the sides of the demijohn, I saw evidence of articraft on Marty's and Martia's part. There was a screen of algae fibre, woven as humans weave cloth or mats—warp and woof in an over-under pattern. The screen was probably designed to provide shade from the sun, which I guess could get fairly strong, even inside the dark glass. The screen was held at the ends by an arrangement of copper wire—the same wire, doubtless that Terry had once dumped into our washbasin aboard the *Searcher*. Old Brunder, with some thought of his own, had put it into the jug. And our friends had used it, demonstrating a primitive culture, beyond which they had no reason to go, except in music.

Now Terry Miklas gave a low, short whistle. Then his talk went rambling, again: "How was it like out here in space, in a world of your own, Marty and Martia? Was it hard to take, or was it peace? And did we just now spoil that? Do you want to return to Mars, or do you want to go much farther? Maybe someday we'll be really able to converse, and you'll be able to tell me how it is with yourself. If you know—as sometimes I think I don't quite know—about me, then you know I think that music is beautiful, restless stuff."

"Go get your harmonica, Terry," Alice urged. "Play something for them…"

Yeah—here was a nice dreamy, young fella, born of various parentage in New York City. And here was my daughter, not too unlike him in background. She had no superlative talent, though she was good at the piano. But then here were a pair of mites, different from them about as completely as was possible—in size, structure, origin; maybe even in basic protoplasm. But between the two halves of this foursome—with almost no other language at all—there was a bond of likeness and understanding.

So I guess that the pattern for the immediate future was already pretty well set, during those few days of returning to Earth. I had to guide the Warrington, being the only one who could still think of routine matters. Terry would be tooting on his mouth organ; then Alice would try it, too. Then Marty or Martia would tinkle a response, sometimes against the sides of the demijohn. Or they'd emerge from it for a while, and tap against something else; sometimes it was notes that they produced, but as often it was words and phrases that they were learning to repeat.

Yes, in this romantic atmosphere of contrasting cultures and mystery, love bloomed very soon between Alice, my daughter, and Terry Miklas. It was a unity of interest and of about everything else that counts, I suppose. How would I know? I was just a mildly cynical but sympathetic outsider, whose consent, if it was needed at all, came about as easily and casually as anything could, two days before we got the Warrington back to the White Sands spaceport:

"Why sure, Terry and Alice."

With that much settled, we got down quickly to another problem.

"Just what happens to Marty and Martia, Dad?" Alice asked.

"Um-m-m—what does?" I enquired. "We have an awful lot of expenses to meet, as we all know. It was expected that our small guests from the Red Planet would be instrumental in defraying them."

"Not if it means selling them like chattels into slavery in a zoo or museum, Dad!" Alice warned. "They are sentient beings—and our friends! Anyhow, there's another way—more lucrative in the long run. Like Terry they're artists. People will want to see them and hear them play—in the theatre. On television…everywhere! All we need is a couple of weeks more—to perfect an act and a program for Marty and Martia, and maybe Terry, too—perhaps even me!"

"Lucrative" was the word that got me most. Yeah, money that means. It was the most reasonable subject that I had heard mentioned in quite a while. And I was proud to know that my daughter had a good, practical head.

Of course there are novelty numbers, and novelty numbers. Some take hold, some don't. The public can be pretty blasé, even when you're dead certain that you have the best thing in the universe. I was sure we couldn't miss, yet I didn't know. Sadly I felt some hopes of at last having a few dollars to rub together possibly being indefinitely postponed. But with both my daughter and my prospective son-in-law gone against the old plan, and with my own self leaning in that direction also, what could I do but stretch my luck a little further?

Terry and Alice got married in White Sands. Then there was a fast scramble for another loan—fortunately small this time. Included in our luggage when we moved to a couple of adobe shacks out in the desert, was a piano and a custom-made case like a suitcase, but with a plastic tank inside.

I lived in the other shack, leaving Alice and Terry and their charge alone a lot. I roamed the nearby hills and kept watch, remembering the recent past. Of course I kept a gun.

Our first try at show business was in Phoenix, Arizona, and all my previous doubts were instantly dissipated. The first agent's eyes fairly bulged at the demonstration performance, and he cussed in wonder. "Maybe you're fibbing about where you got these fish," he said. "But do I care?"

The sound-truck that belonged to a big local theatre of dignity was in the streets twenty minutes later, announcing solemnly: "A special fifteen-minute feature will extend our evening program to 11:45 p.m. This is to introduce something sincerely unheard of by us before today. Something completely charming from another world—Mars, we are told. Beyond this, words may fail us, or seem crudely sensational. Therefore, come and discover for yourselves."

So that night, Marty and Martia performed to a packed house, and incidentally, to a far larger television audience.

I guess the basic framework of the program was corny. Terry Miklas was a rather shy and awkward master of ceremonies, keeping his harmonica and guitar with him to draw out and encourage Marty and Martia with his own music. Alice, at the piano, stayed in the background for the same purpose.

When Terry and Alice began to play, the star performers scrambled up a little wooden ladder and out of their tank, which was set on a table, and proceeded to enjoy themselves more or less extemporaneously on all the apparatus that had been arranged for them. *Home Sweet Home* came out on steel strings stretched over a sounding board, and on a tumbler, in unison. But it was the only number that they played that anybody except Alice, Terry, and myself had ever heard before.

VERY SOON Marty and Martia were performing alone—funny, dainty, intent little monsters, the color of patinaed gild, and as beautiful as a childhood fancy. Now they were at the steel strings and the tumbler; now their claws vibrated a small drum, while they crouched on its head. Now their flippers were cupped against pieces of resonant wood.

Their music was faint and weird and aching, and it seemed to reach out endlessly with its eerie richness. The amplifier system took something away from it, until very soon Terry Miklas turned it off. Then, among those thousands of people in the audience, you could have heard a pin drop. I was out there; I knew.

Marty and Martia played for seven minutes; then they retired independently to their tank, to freshen their gills. But back in the water, they didn't stop entertaining. They made the sides of the tank vibrate, pronouncing words that they knew:

"Hhelllo-o-o! Wwe-ee arrr-r ffrrom-m Mmarrzz! Yuuu arrr-r owwrr ff'rrennzzz…!" they buzzed.

Some of this I shouldn't bother to tell. It is old now, and everybody heard at the time. The reports about Marty and Martia, who had no other names that we ever found out, went everywhere. And later performances were no less enthusiastically received than the one of that first night, when at times the audience was as quiet as the dead. At others, it roared with laughter, or brought the house down with applause. Encores extended that first show to fully three times its allotted fifteen minutes. The important play that preceded Marty's and Martia's act was almost forgotten.

As the people got up to leave, I listened to the various comments—pleased, endearing, and comic. A surprising number of folks didn't believe what they had seen and heard.

"Trick stuff, sure, but I like good tricks," a fat man announced to a pal. "Ever hear the old joke about the drunk, the mouse pianist, and the miniature piano…?"

At supper in our hotel after the show, Alice's and Terry's faces shone like a couple of bright new pennies.

"We made it!" Terry Miklas said jubilantly. "Or rather—they did! It's an avalanche! I wonder if they appreciate all the flowers they got…"

"What I'm trying to do is pin down exactly the secret of their success," I offered. "Of course I know—I *feel* the answer coming to me from all sides. But how do you get all of it into words? Let's see—well—in the first, place their music would still be beautiful even if it was well-known instead of being completely novel. Then they're the only actual *sentient* beings—I think we can say that it is proven now that they are that, can't we?—other than Genus Homo of Earth that anyone has ever seen. Then, behind them, is the mystic glamor of ancient Mars. A lot of the rest is whimsy. They're like little characters in a myth or legend which can't be, but that we all wish for. Yet they are—unbelievably—real..."

"Yes, Dad!" Alice broke in eagerly. "I hardly supposed that a rough spaceman like you ever thought along such lines! But you've got it pretty well stated. They have some of the charm of the Lorelei, and of fairy princesses and ruined castles and immortal woodland sprites and lost treasures—maybe even of Santa Claus! And they're *real!* They're a thing that our hard civilization wants and needs to rest itself—a little of special poetry, music, and magic! They're a very unique blend..."

Well that night a dozen would-be sponsors discovered that possible remarks like "We're from Mars" could be made to rhyme with something about stars, and—just for example—some manufacturer's candy bars. The idea of course was to make up commercial jingles and have Marty and Martia vibrate them out in words and tinkles. I guess it could have been done without much difficulty. But I felt very sour to the idea right away, as did Terry and Alice.

"We know that what we've got is good," I told these gentlemen. "We don't mean ever to corn it up."

No, I don't think we lost a thing here by taking a firm stand. In fact I believe we gained in quality and respect.

From Phoenix we swung west, performing in Los Angeles, San Francisco, and Seattle. Then we moved east again, to Minneapolis, and south to St. Louis and

New Orleans, and up to Chicago and Detroit and Cleveland, and on to New York. By then the names of Marty and Martia were up in lighted letters so big that you could have flown our old freighter, the *Searcher,* right through them. Three brief weeks of this kind of glory we had in all. For the time being, we were cleaning up in a very practical manner. But in the long run the pair that was our bonanza turned out to be fool's gold. From the beginning, my memory and a hunch kept informing me that even those three weeks were borrowed time. Something bad just had to happen.

CHAPTER SIX

It was I who suggested a vacation up on the Maine coast. It was a hot July then. Terry and Alice agreed quickly. But I think that what we all wanted was not so much a rest, but, subconsciously, a place to entrench for trouble. Of course the subconscious mind isn't always very logical. The Maine coast was no shelter against the legal suit that was what I expected mostly—not that any of us minded paying off. But trouble—when you feel sure that it is on the way but can't tell at what moment or just how it will make itself known—can be magnified into a nebulous phantom that frightens the deep, primitive part of a person. A legal contact could be one approach. But there could be others. Someone at night, for instance. With this in mind, we had hired two armed guards.

As matters turned out, we were taken by surprise for one vital instant. It was a summer dusk, soft and rich. The day before, we had made an interesting discovery—final proof of Martia's femininity. Visible within her small, semi-transparent body, were a dozen tiny and incomplete duplicates of Marty and herself.

Alice was still smiling over this fact, there in the kitchen. Terry and I were also present, enjoying a pair of beers. The door to the garden was open. Fifty yards away a brook babbled. The Atlantic was half a mile distant. Right behind my chair, on another small table, was Marty's and Martia's plastic tank.

We heard footsteps grinding on pebbles, I turned, seeing dimly someone approaching from the garden—a man in slacks and checkered shirt and a hat. It could have been Mills, one of the guards, or a farmer neighbor. I know now that back among the trees he must have been waiting—waiting for a moment when neither Mills nor Davis (the other guard) were in front of our kitchen door. He came right on into the kitchen without a greeting, and in a startling instant he stood as close as I was to Marty's and Martia's tank, and in a better position to take hold of it.

Not till then did we realize who he was. I guess we were too used to seeing him in the coverall of a spaceman. Besides, his scraggy whiskers were shaved off.

While Terry and I were scrambling furiously and defensively to our feet, he grinned kind of self-consciously, and said, "Hello, Durbin and Miklas. Weren't you expecting me sometime? I guess I have certain rights of discovery, concerning these sensational beings, too. Financial ones, anyway."

Brunder's big hairy mitt was curved around that transparent tank. That was a bad circumstance all around. My thought then was that he was talking about money, for which I acknowledge respect. Though where Marty and Martia were concerned, I realized more fully now that it wasn't the main thing with me. When we had returned to White Sands from space, after performing a rescue, I hadn't worried too much about Brunder, feeling that his own nefarious attempt to grab the *Pisces Martia* for himself alone was too dangerously fresh for him to try legal action against us. But now that incident was a fading memory, and we had begun to look rich, and hence possibly guilty in the eyes of the world. So I was more wary, now. Maybe I misjudged him, but my further thought was still that Brunder just wasn't the kind to have any control over our small friends, whatsoever.

So I was all swift and perhaps ill-advised defensive action. I grabbed that tank, and he took hold of it tighter, and Terry leapt close to help me. For a second we all tussled; then all three of us went down on the floor. The tank, which we all still clutched, was overturned; its wire top came off, and its contents sloshed violently...

Alice gave an almost agonized cry. Terry said, "Damn!" I used stronger language than that as I picked myself up for further action. But the last that any of us saw of Marty and Martia were them scrambling away like mice into the thickening shadows of the garden.

"You numbskulls!" Brunder yelled sheepishly. "What in hell did you start messing with me for? All I wanted was to talk about my just rights, privately, letting bygones be bygones. Now look what happened!"

Our worthy ex-captain had a point there, I had to admit to myself—withal a doubtful one. But I had plenty of counterpoints of my own.

"Why didn't you announce yourself like a man instead of sneaking around and barging in like a cockroach, Brunder!" I hollered back at him. "You could have had your stinking share of the money we got from the programs! For all I mind, you can still have it, and be damned!"

He looked glumly furious, but said no more just then. He and I followed Terry and Alice out into the garden where they were calling, "Marty!" and "Martia!" But the only answer in the young night was the sleepy and lonely chirp of the crickets, and the babble of the brook nearby.

"That's it," Brunder grumbled. "They would naturally have aimed for the water, wouldn't they?"

"Bright man, ain't you?" I snapped at him sarcastically.

"Knothead, yourself, Durbin!" he snarled.

"I've a hunch that they'd make right for the ocean, via the creek," Terry Miklas said musingly. "Hey—let's all get in the car and drive down there right away!"

So that was what we did, leaving the guards at the house. What practical good the excursion was supposed to accomplish, I don't know. At the abrupt rocky shore, the brook became narrow and deep and gushing—no place to look for two small fishlike creatures, though we tried that futilely with flashlights. A big white moon was rising out over the Atlantic, its light making a twinkling path on the waves. Millions of years ago the ocean must have been dreamy and enigmatic like this, as no doubt it still would be for millions of years to come.

We all walked along the shore, looking out at the water helplessly. At last Terry Miklas started one of his absentminded soliloquies:

"Maybe the sea was what they wanted, what they came with us for. On Mars there haven't been any real seas for much longer than you can imagine. Trans-spatial migrants searching for a thing only dimly left in their race-memories—was that what they were…? We wanted to take care of you, Marty and Martia. But I guess you didn't feel free. Well, good luck. But the Atlantic is awfully big and dark and deep. I hope you don't get into trouble in it…"

After a minute, Alice asked sadly: "Well—what do we do now?"

"One thing we can do," I growled, "is get back to the house and figure up what old stinker Brunder here thinks we owe him, and pay him off so he'll go away where we won't have to look at him anymore. It's worth the price."

Mr. Brunder looked furious again, but maybe sort of hurt, too.

"Don't worry, Durbin," he snarled in return. "I wouldn't want anything that you thought was yours around me to make me itch! So you'll get a deduction of a few thousand from your check to me—to cover yours and Miklas' share of that load of algae brought from Mars in the *Searcher*."

"Ah—now it's Mr. Generosity, huh?" I sneered at him. "Listen, Brunder—I wouldn't let you forget that algae, or our share, or who did most of the work…"

It's funny how people are. I hated Brunder less now than I used to; yet I was riding him harder.

At the house I made out his check. He said, "Thanks," and stalked away with awkward pride, which somehow made me recall how he used to scratch the back of Toby, that old tomcat of his, and of how once— have I even mentioned that before this?—I thought I'd heard him croon to Marty and Martia when he had them behind the locked doors of his cabin aboard the *Searcher*.

But we sure had gotten on each other's nerves during that trip!

When he was gone I said to my daughter and son-in-law:

"So is this the end of our strangest adventure?"

"I don't know, Popeye," Terry answered. "But I don't see how it could be. Because we don't know just what happened, or will happen, to our star performers. The adventure will go on, incomplete, until we find out. Or until somebody else finds out. And if nobody does, it'll go on forever."

CHAPTER SEVEN

The newscast people were out at dawn, and the news was given to the world. I guess most people remember. Right then some big commercial enterprises were exploring the cold moons of Jupiter, and beginning the hardheaded job of exploiting the mineral deposits there; but folks forgot all that for a little while. For their whimsical interests were drawn to a half-legend that had vanished again into the unknown, or had slipped into a new phase, leaving behind the memory of its reality. A million things were said by millions of people, and though the words might be different, the message was usually about the same. Here, a realistic, sometimes cruel populace, charmed by something little and different, paused to be kind:

"Good luck, Marty and Martia, wherever you've gone. And may we meet again…"

Oh, there was some fear, too—perhaps not entirely unreasonable. One newspaper headline went something like this:

"SUPER FISH FROM MARS INVADE OCEANS. WITH INTELLIGENCE OF HUMAN LEVEL, WILL THEY MULTIPLY, MAKE PLANS? WHAT UNKNOWN DANGERS LIE AHEAD?"

These were thoughts that subsided as months passed, and the Atlantic remained unchanged and the story of a brief visitation dimmed somewhat in most minds—Terry's and Alice's and mine not included.

Terry Miklas had early offers to go on making music for the public. He turned them all down.

"What they remember of me, Popeye," he said later, "is that I was one of those who introduced Marty and Martia. People want to hear and see me for that reason—which doesn't make my music worth listening to in its own right—at least not yet. Besides, I've got to keep watch along the shore here. Because you-know-who may want to come back…"

When I thought about it, Terry's purpose applied as well to Alice and me. Because Marty and Martia had been just about the biggest event in our lives.

We had expected to have a lot of money. When our debts were paid we were quite a ways from being broke, but we were down to an economy level. We kept the house we had rented there on the Maine coast. Now our watch began. Fishermen were keeping their eyes open, too, thinking that their nets might bring up one or both of the runaways, or maybe some of their progeny. But nothing like that ever happened, as far as we know. Though of course here was something to add to the numerous and ancient legends of the sea.

During those autumn days and evenings, Terry would walk alone along the rocky shore, or with Alice, or with both Alice and me; and he'd play on his harmonica—capturing some of the mood of the eerie music that we had all heard. He got better at it as time went on, but improvement wasn't his first motive.

"Maybe my tooting will draw those darn fools back!" he'd growl.

The vigil went on into the winter, when the Atlantic was often really something to watch—huge white breakers swirling and thundering in and roaring like devils. I suppose that Terry Miklas' patrolling of the shore—blowing weird tunes on his mouth organ—in weather like that will make another yarn of the sea; a folktale of peculiar devotion that will last for centuries along that coast.

But there were also occasions of quiet and fog—like that one evening in January. In this mild weather, all three of us were out there along the shore again. Far out we heard the bell of a buoy clanking sleepily. And Terry tooted on his mouth organ again—little dreamy, coaxing bursts and trills that no human besides himself could have produced.

Suddenly he stopped, and cocked his head to one side eagerly, listening. Alice and I did the same.

"Hear that?" Terry whispered at last, tensely.

"Yes, Terry—yes!" Alice answered.

"I think so," I put in. "Wait... Shhh..."

Just for a second the slurring, questioning notes were there, dim but unmistakable—coming from among the nearby rocks.

But when we had scrambled to the water's edge, there just wasn't any more music, though Terry Miklas blew and blew on his harmonica. The sounds of a miniature xylophone had faded for good. Our flashlights, boring through the fog, revealed only many seashells among the rocks.

"A shell," Alice mused.

"They're alive, anyway—at least one of them is—the perverse ingrates!" Terry growled, but his face looked pleased. "They could have returned to us, but they didn't... Well, we all love freedom, so I suppose that any inspirational thing of legend has to be free."

Again I felt chilly, yet pleasantly haunted. How many charming myths have been pursued during the course of history? The Grail of the Knights. The Fairy Morgana. The Fountain of Youth. And now something else that we remembered as real.

Our watch continued there beside the Atlantic, which often is magnificent enough to thrill even a professional spaceman. Winter ended and Spring began; still there were no new signs of those we sought.

BUT IN mid-May events took some fresh turns. The first of these was sour. While we wandered along the shore, we saw a hulking figure scanning the rocks, some hundreds of yards farther along the water's edge.

I nodded toward the man and remarked, "So we've got company once more. Brunder has been drawn back here, too."

He waved at us mockingly, and then moved off at his leisure in the opposite direction.

The next incident was much more of a romantic order. Terry and I were on that rough beach again, early one morning. We must have known every pebble and shell for miles each way by now. But suddenly there was a glint at our feet; in the sunrise it shone yellow and metallic. I was sure that it hadn't been there the evening before.

Terry picked it up, and held it in his hand. It was a tiny golden brooch with antique griffons on it, eroded by the sea. There was no doubt that the thing was centuries old.

Terry looked speculative, and something greedy and ancient ached in my nerves. "Once there were pirates," Terry said. "Is that the answer for this—or part of it?"

Neither of us craved Brunder's company, just then. But suddenly there he was, smirking at us.

"I've got as much right to be here as anybody, Durbin," he pointed out to me. "You found something, you two, didn't you?"

"What's it to you if we did, Brunder?" I snapped at him.

"Nothin'," he replied with forced mildness and a shrug. "Except that so did I find something."

He opened his paw, and a compelling curiosity made me look inside it. He had a tiny lump of yellow metal that showed signs of having been stamped with a numeral or something once, though this was too worn to decipher, now.

"It's heavy, Durbin," Brunder said. "I went down there by those rocks, and there it was."

Terry and I were stuck with a swapping of courtesies, so to speak. So Terry opened his palm, too.

Brunder looked. Then he looked at me. "Gold ain't worth what it used to be in the old days, Durbin," he said. "There are too many sources of it now, in space. But it's still worth quite a bit. And there are other more valuable things on the sea floor. I wonder if you are thinking of the same thing that I am, Durbin? That if a man had a small friend with special skills... Well, skip it, Durbin. See you around. Come on, Toby..."

Yes—there on a rock was that big tomcat of Brunder's, glaring expectantly at the water, his tail lashing. Brunder had to call again to make him come away.

NOW AND for weeks to come, Terry and Alice and I practically lived on the beach, for we had seen what might be a further sign. Terry blew on his mouth organ intermittently, hour after hour. Alice threw bits of bread on the ocean—it was something that Marty and Martin had liked. But the crying seagulls grabbed most of it. And the pair from Mars who had left us made no attempt to see their old friends.

But every morning when we pulled ourselves out of our sleeping bags on the shore—every morning for ten days—we always found something that hadn't been on the beach the night previous. Always the objects were in the same little, less rocky stretch of shore, fifty yards long—as if to make them easier to find.

Twice we found two medium-sized pearls. Once it was the link of a golden chain, and a cut ruby. Several mornings yielded a pair of golden coins, too worn to identify. Delivery was usually in pairs. It got so that whenever we didn't find two of something, we figured that Brunder must have found its other companion piece.

One dawn we thought we heard the xylophone. Later, in the sunshine, we were sure we glimpsed a flash of green and gold, thirty yards out from the rocks.

"Something really ought to happen soon," Alice said that day. "I wouldn't be surprised if they were back with us by tomorrow. And have you two decided yet whence came all the things of treasure—and how?"

She was kidding. The answer was more or less obvious, wasn't it? I thought of two small beings from Mars, lugging gifts up from the undersea in their flippers.

"Marty and Martia were with us long enough to begin to understand humans," I chuckled. "Maybe they feel obligated to us. Or maybe these presents are peace offerings for their running away. Or perhaps tribute is being paid to Earthly music and friends."

To myself I thought of the ocean—little known to me beyond looking at its surface, except from pictures. The sunlight turning violet deep down, and then fading to blackness more awesome than that of space. Submerged mountains and unexplored valleys. Hidden wealth. The skeletons of ships. Beautiful gardens of anemones. Weird, fantastic world. The monsters of the deeps. Could Marty and Martia go even there—letting the fluids of their flesh become gradually compressed, until it thus assumed an internal counter pressure to hold back the terrible weight of the ocean above, and keep them from being crushed? Perhaps they could. For it was said that even warm-blooded whales, accustomed to the surface, could dive hundreds of fathoms deep. And to defend themselves against enemies, our Martian pair and their probable offspring had their stings and their intelligence.

Alice's optimism about a possible reunion the next day proved less than groundless. For the first time in many mornings we found nothing of value on the shore. Week followed week, and it was the same. There were no more gifts, and no more indications of any kind that the creatures Terry and I had found on the Red Planet were still somewhere off the coast.

July passed, and half of August. In spite of the gifts from the sea—of limited value—our funds were getting low. I felt that we had about reached the end of a phase, for good.

And we used to think that we'd get rich!

Oh, sure. I was aware of a lot of time wasted instead. Yet I felt sad in another way, too.

Terry and Alice also looked sad. But now they received some offers to play for people again. Terry did have a lot of talent. Marty and Martia had given him something completely new, and he had developed adding elements of his own.

As for me, I'm an active sort. I couldn't just hang around forever. For one thing, space was beckoning me back. So I said, "Well, kids, when do we break this up?"

"Soon I guess, Dad," Alice answered. "It's been a whole year. But we'll always have to check back here now and then."

"Yeah, honey," I agreed.

CHAPTER EIGHT

Perhaps it was queer, but Brunder was still around. But Marty and Martia had been the big thing in his life, too; so he was just as persistent as we were. Maybe he thought that something might still break, and give him what is supposed to be at the end of the rainbow. He was living up in the village, somewhere. I glimpsed him, with that cat of his, along the shore. And quite often I saw Toby roaming by himself. He knew Terry and me, and he'd come to the house; Alice would give him a handout.

So Toby became the key to a vital point. You know the affinity that cats and dogs have for smelly objects. I saw Toby one morning at the back of our garden by the brook. He had something in his mouth. It consisted of two long ropy ends, connected by a slender cord. Yeah—nameless refuse you'd say it was.

But something about it—I didn't know what—aroused my interest. So I approached Toby, and he growled a warning.

"Steady, Tomcat," I said. "Do you expect to chew through whatever that is? It looks pretty tough."

He growled again, and made his fur, which was marked like a tiger's, bristle. But now I got a better look at what he had. The two club-like ends of the object seemed to be composed of a mixture of clay and fibre, cemented together. It could be brook-clay, and the cellulose from aquatic plants.

After that, my blood began to pound, and I was in no mood to let Toby argue with me. "Thanks, Tomcat," I said. "Remind me to give you a whole steak sometime. But—come on—now—I want *that!*"

I got a clawed hand out of the deal; Toby got a swat on his ear, for which I should apologize.

I felt of the two tapered objects—joined together like two old friends who didn't want to lose each other. Then I hollered:

"Terry! Alice! Come here quick…!"

We put what Toby had found into a plastic tank that had been empty for a year. We poured water shallowly over it. Then we waited and drank pots of coffee, and paced up and down and speculated.

"They must have swum up the brook from the ocean," Terry said. "After that, scrambling overland among so much unfamiliar vegetation, maybe they got lost trying to find our house. It's been hot and dry most of this summer—really hot for anything Martian. Besides, Marty and Martia are mainly aquatic. They can't live out of water forever, and even the brook is almost dry this far from the sea. But they had a Martian way to keep alive—no, there are certain fish in African rivers that encase themselves in mud during the season when there is almost no water… Anyway—dammit—I hope that now everything is as fine as it seems!"

Just about everything was fine. By noon that day, Marty and Martia were out of their cocoons, swimming in their tank and trilling out our names and words that they hadn't forgotten, apparently delighted to be in our company again, after a year of complete freedom in an ocean of a strange, alien planet:

"Hhelllo-o-o-o, Tterrreee! Aaalllizzz! Ppoppaiee-ee...! Thhhannkzzz! Wweee cumm baaaackkkk...!"

Yes—the legend had returned. I got on the phone. Minutes later the world knew about it. I guess most everyone remembers how it was. Within an hour we were swamped with newscast people, and sponsors, and representatives from every phase of the entertainment industry. Also, there were serious scientists. It looked like the bonanza once more—but bigger than ever.

But Terry didn't want to sign any contracts. I thought that he must have gained in practical worldly knowledge, and was playing hard to get—a smart thing to do, with what we had.

"Give us a couple of weeks' time, to see about several matters," was what he said to the commercial and television and theatrical people.

Alice and he proceeded to teach Marty and Martia a larger vocabulary. "They're folks, as far as we are concerned," he reminded me. "They have the intelligence and feelings of folks. And this time they must understand us and speak well enough to tell us what they want—as is their right."

While admitting some suspicions of more frustrations on the way, I found myself agreeing with all this. It couldn't be otherwise.

So at last Terry put it to them. "What'll it be, friends?" he asked. "Do you want to go traveling and making music with us, again? Or are you homesick for the northern icecap of Mars, under the dark blue sky? I know that you must be as restless as your music, or is it something else that you want? There are many possible places and situations. There is even the zoo, or the museum—though I don't think I'd recommend either..."

No—Marty and Martia didn't answer right away. First they touched fins there in their tank. Then they swam around each other in a kind of dance. Finally Marty put his flippers against the plastic of the tank, and words buzzed out:

"Nnottt nnowww Mmarrrzz orrr ttrraavvellll...Bbbetterrr nneww thhinnngzzz...Ttryy zzzooo...Ttryy mmuuzzeeummm...."

"Zoo? Museum?" Terry protested. "But that'll be like prison, Marty!"

"Zzoo—Mmuuzzeeum!" Marty persisted, and Martia echoed his words.

"You don't know what you're talking about!"

I'M AFRAID Terry Miklas was prejudiced. He didn't want to lose Marty and Martia as his tour-partners. I don't think it was the money so much—not with him. Rather, it was like having close friends who choose a separate path, and so are partly lost.

Now Alice put in her two cents worth. "Maybe they don't know what they're talking about, Terry," she said. "Who does...when they try something new—especially so new as the ways of another planet? Marty and Martia have to find out things for themselves. So, from their view-point, you could be wrong."

Well, Terry Miklas had a nice mild grin in defeat. He shrugged. "All right. Music from Polar Mars," he said.

"My very best wishes, and we'll still see each other around."

Then he looked at me, and the look said something that I'd already sensed. We used to talk about selling the *Pisces Martis* to zoos or museums or big scientific organizations for a heavy price. It was still possible, as far as such institutions and so forth were concerned. Funds were no doubt available. And I don't think that Marty and Martia would have minded being exchanged for money in the least, nor would have felt in the least enslaved, thereby. For it is known now that money to them is just a quaint human custom, not influencing their liberty an iota. But still we had our own ethics to follow—rigid and necessary for us. We did not sell a humanly intelligent friend as a chattel. To do so was now unthinkable. Wherever Marty and Martia went, they went by their own choice, as responsible individuals. So again, for us, the Bonanza had to slip away.

Everybody knows how it has been. Marty and Martia are in New York, now—in the Museum of Natural History. But they've been flown around to many cities. They have a big tank, now, full of Martian and Earthly aquatic plants, and a hundred gadgets for Marty to fool with and examine, and for them both to tinkle out their haunting tunes on. Their ancestors couldn't have lived more luxuriously, even in the days of Mars' ancient glory. Scientists from everywhere keep studying them and asking them questions. They even have books printed on waterproof parchment. It seems that their special attendant, Professor Harwind, is teaching them to read. And so, for the time being at least, their carefree, primitive existence, colored only by music, has been tainted by civilized industriousness.

Children love them, of course, and love the eerie trills and soaring, elfin chords, as of a tiny xylophone that often speaks with words, too. But even tough spacemen, fresh from the mines of Callisto or Ganymede, come to watch and listen and wonder. And everyone else has seen and heard—if only by television and recording. Yes, there is something gentle and fascinating about the legendary mood that is Marty and Martia—even when it is pinned down, to be easily examined.

Alice and Terry? They struck out on their own, and are already a famous musical couple in their own right— making something new and fresh and truly their own, out of the art they borrowed. Perhaps it is final satisfaction and the end of restlessness for Terry Miklas. But sometimes they go back to see Marty and Martia, and put on a joint show with them, for the kids who come to the museum.

But I remember one time—not so very long ago, it was—when I dropped in to the museum to see Marty and Martia, as I still do quite often. They understood and spoke human language a lot better by then, being quick to learn. So I said: "Suckers. Sloths. Cooped up here. Independence sold for comfort. Shame! A legend must be free…"

"Ssommtimme wwee g go-o," Marty buzzed on the glass of the tank in answer. "Whennn neww thhinnggzz callll… Wwe arrr alllwwayzz ffrreeee…"

I guess Marty is right. When they want out, they'll say so. Popular opinion is on their side. And if this weren't so, they still have the cleverness to escape. To be a little like animals on display doesn't hurt their pride at all. By the way people like them and react to them, they are like prisoners who can walk through walls—if they are prisoners at all. Besides, they have plenty of time. Scientists, questioning them, have found that their life span is something more than three hundred Earth-years. So sometime they'll wander away again.

Marty said something more to me that time: "Ssuckkerr! Mmenn expllorr ddisstanttt pplannettzzz. Fforgggett ddeeeppp oshhunn. Sstranngge."

I took the hint. In fact the idea had been revolving in my mind for some time. First I bought some recordings of Marty's and Martia's music, right there in the museum store. Guess who I found there? Yeah—Brunder. Oh, yes—he'd been around at the house up in Maine after Marty and Martia got back. "Hi, Durbin," he said without rancor.

I felt lonesome. Besides, there was something in the air—like the lion lying down with the lamb, maybe. Or would you say instead that we were just a couple of old goats?

"I got an idea, Brunder," I said. "Maybe sometime I'll get rich after all."

"Possibly I got the same idea, Durbin," Brunder intimated. "I also bought some used deep-sea diving equipment—cheap. Now if you could scrape enough money together to buy or rent us an old launch, someplace…"

Well, in a matter of a week or so, Brunder and I were off the Maine coast together. We were a couple of grouchy old spacemen, trying a new racket that intrigued us. Toby, the tomcat, was dozing in the engine room. We had an underwater sound system, through which we were playing some elfin music, which originated on another planet.

I went down a rope in a deep-sea diving suit that is a little like a spacesuit, but is two hundred times as heavy. When I had been down there about an hour, I met a little green and gold critter who liked what our sound-system was playing, looked like some old friends of ours, though he wasn't full grown, yet, and clearly wanted to be friendly.

Oh, we had to converse with him on a number of occasions, give him the legendary name of Neptune, and teach him some English words. But pretty soon he got the idea of what we wanted, and led us right to the broken strong-box of an old, sunken sailing ship. Then he found us another vessel. The take in antique jewelry and money wasn't very great, but it kept us going.

We kept working at the salvage business, with Neptune as our locator. We even conversed with him about another legend—the one about Lost Atlantis—but he doesn't have any information.

Finally, however, we had a heavy bathyspheric submarine built, atom-powered, for real deep-sea diving. Yeah—funny how when space travel began, people forgot about the strange rich world of the deep ocean. Because down there, with Neptune's assistance, we have tapped about the richest deposit of uranium ore that has ever been found any planet.

THE END

www.ingramcontent.com/pod-product-compliance
Lightning Source LLC
Chambersburg PA
CBHW030310180626
46810CB00003B/1001